Crawford wrapped a protective arm around Mateus's shoulders when he started to shake. The warmth was grounding, like Crawford might be able to physically keep him in place. "Detention center? Can't we just wait here? I can have a lawyer on the phone in under a minute. You can't arrest him just for being here."

Could he really? Or was that just a bluff? Either way, it was comforting.

"I'm sorry, sir, but Mr. Fontes has no legal claim to stay in either country. He's in violation of the terms of his visa, and he'll be arrested for it. Immigration fraud is a serious crime."

The man still seemed sympathetic, but there was a note of steel in his voice. Mateus hadn't really thought of trying to re-up his visa as fraud, but apparently the government had a different view.

Crawford's arm tightened around his shoulders, his fingers digging into Mateus's arm.

"He does have a legal right to be in this country. He's my fiancé, and I'm an American citizen."

WELCOME TO

Dear Reader,

Love is the dream. It dazzles us, makes us stronger, and brings us to our knees. Dreamspun Desires tell stories of love featuring your favorite heartwarming heroes, captivating plots, and exotic locations. Stories that make your breath catch and your imagination soar.

In the pages of these wonderful love stories, readers can escape to a world where love conquers all, the tenderness of a first kiss sweeps you away, and your heart pounds at the sight of the one you love.

When you put it all together, you find romance in its truest form.

Love always finds a way.

Elizabeth North

Executive Director
Dreamspinner Press

Bru Baker

Tall, Dark, and Deported

Helen, I love you! I'm so glad you're in my life. ♡ Bru

DREAMSPUN DESIRES

PUBLISHED BY

Published by
DREAMSPINNER PRESS

5032 Capital Circle SW, Suite 2, PMB# 279,
Tallahassee, FL 32305-7886 USA
www.dreamspinnerpress.com

This is a work of fiction. Names, characters, places, and incidents either are the product of author imagination or are used fictitiously, and any resemblance to actual persons, living or dead, business establishments, events, or locales is entirely coincidental.

ISBN: 978-1-63477-683-7
Digital ISBN: 978-1-63477-684-4
Library of Congress Control Number: 2016913744
Published April 2017
v. 1.0

Printed in the United States of America

This paper meets the requirements of
ANSI/NISO Z39.48-1992 (Permanence of Paper).

BRU BAKER got her first taste of life as a writer at the tender age of four, when she started publishing a weekly newspaper for her family. What they called nosiness she called a nose for news, and no one was surprised when she ended up with degrees in journalism and political science and started a career in journalism.

Bru spent more than a decade writing for newspapers before making the jump to fiction. She now works in reference and readers' advisory in a Midwestern library, though she still finds it hard to believe someone's willing to pay her to talk about books all day. Most evenings you can find her curled up with a book or her laptop. Whether it's creating her own characters or getting caught up in someone else's, there's no denying that Bru is happiest when she's engrossed in a story. She and her husband have two children, which means a lot of her books get written from the sidelines of various sports practices.

Website: www.bru-baker.com

Blog: www.bru-baker.blogspot.com

Twitter: @bru_baker

Facebook: www.facebook.com/bru.baker79

Goodreads: www.goodreads.com/author/show/6608093.Bru_Baker

E-mail: bru@bru-baker.com

Chapter One

“**IT** wasn’t a request, Crawford. Helena has booked you on a plane to Vancouver next week, and I expect you to be on it.”

Crawford kept his features carefully blank, his gaze focused just over his boss’s shoulder on the Warhol that hung behind him. It had been hideously expensive, especially given it was gracing the wall of a man who didn’t even like art. Crawford had been the one sent to the auction to bid on it. George had claimed it was exactly the type of statement piece that belonged in the office of the chairman of a highly successful international boutique hotel chain.

Not that attending art auctions was technically part of his job. But lately, George had been expanding Crawford’s job description more and more to justify sending him on ridiculous errands like flying across the country to attend an auction with the company's interior designer.

Crawford focused on the garish painting and prayed for patience. His pulse had been racing ever since George had announced, in front of the entire board, that Crawford would be heading up the audit of the company's flagship Canadian hotel. The announcement itself wasn't a surprise. The Vancouver property had been in a downward spiral for the past few quarters, the numbers not quite adding up and certainly not keeping pace with the gains in the company's other North American locations—nowhere close to the projections Crawford himself had been part of setting. And since Crawford was the company's top auditor and management consultant, he'd been expecting the assignment.

Given the size of the undertaking, it also wasn't that much of a surprise to hear that he'd be part of a team of auditors instead of going solo like he often did.

And if it had been one of the half-dozen North American consultants he'd worked with before, he would have been at his desk even now, poring over the reports to ready himself for the trip. But the CEO was bringing in Crawford's counterpart from the European office to collaborate, and that was a deal breaker. George knew exactly what he was asking by sending Crawford there. Hell, everyone at Chatham-Thompson knew why Crawford gave the European headquarters and all communication with his counterpart there a wide berth. It wasn't like Crawford and Davis had hidden their relationship. They'd been together three years. Half of the company's executives had come to their wedding, for Christ's sake.

Crawford grimaced, rubbing a hand over his jaw. One of the last civil things Davis had said to him was that he hoped there were no hard feelings about him taking the promotion that would move him halfway across the world. As if their marriage had meant nothing. As if their time together had just been Davis biding his time before climbing the next rung on the corporate ladder.

Needless to say, Crawford hadn't been quite so cordial about it. Following several disastrous conference calls, the other execs realized the importance of scheduling meetings with Crawford and Davis separately and had been careful to do so.

Until now.

"George, Edward has offered to oversee the audit," Crawford said. "And, respectfully, you really don't need both Davis and me on this. It makes much more sense to have a more junior auditor who's familiar with the property there to help Davis run the numbers and talk to the staff. He and I together would be overkill."

Crawford was proud of the way his voice didn't shake. His hands were the only part of him to break rank and tremble, but they were tightened into fists in his lap, hidden from view by George's enormous oak desk.

"Edward is perfectly capable," George agreed with a deceptive calm that always preceded his most unpopular edicts. Crawford's mentor was eerily good at reading people and pushing them past their comfort zones in the name of professional growth. His stomach sank. This smacked of George's special brand of meddling. "I'll be frank with you, Crawford. This is definitely something one of the junior members on your team could handle. The interviews and on-site data gathering, at least. But I thought this would be a chance for you to prove to the board that you are serious about your future here at Chatham-Thompson."

Crawford ground his teeth together. He'd been working for this company for more than half his life, starting as a desk clerk with all the other college grunts, graduating to the concierge desk at the biggest hotel in the chain within two years. Before long, he'd been promoted to the corporate offices, working grueling eighty-hour weeks while simultaneously getting his MBA. It had paid off too. He'd earned himself a vice presidency by the time he was thirty-four.

"I am serious about Chatham-Thompson. Don't be ridiculous," Crawford snapped.

Crawford had given his entire life to the company. Horrendously long workweeks, years where he'd let his vacation time slide by unclaimed because he was too busy building the company to take it—ironic, since he worked for the largest resort hotel chain in the world. He was the most dedicated employee in the executive offices after George. He just didn't see the need to force himself to work with his ex-husband to prove it.

"It's a done deal, Crawford," George said. "I know it's hard, but it's been three years. You need to get past it. I've indulged your feud for too long, and now it's starting to affect the bottom line. I can't let that happen." George stood to signify the end of the conversation. "Your flight has been scheduled. I'm assuming you'll stay on-property like you usually do?"

Crawford was too numb to do anything but nod in agreement. He'd been railroaded, and his chest felt like it had met the train head-on.

"Excellent. Helena will send all the details to your administrative assistant. We'll schedule a conference call once you've set up shop and done your preliminary survey."

George dropped his gaze to the tablet in front of him, an obvious dismissal. He'd said his piece, and even while Crawford's world was crumbling around him, George remained coolly unaware.

Crawford wanted to argue, to put his foot down and refuse, but he was afraid he'd lose that particular game of chicken. Would George really fire him over this? Was avoiding Davis really worth flushing his entire career down the toilet?

Not for the first time, Crawford wondered what his life would have been like if he'd never taken the first promotion that launched him into corporate. He'd been happy as a concierge, daydreaming about running his own hotel someday. Even now his favorite part of his job was getting out into the hotels and working with guests. He didn't get to do it too often anymore, and when he did, it was usually dealing with disgruntled customers who were staying at failing properties. But it was still miles better than sitting in a stuffy office looking at budget line items.

George looked up, his brow raised like he was surprised to see Crawford still in his office. "Are we clear?"

Crawford didn't even try for a smile as he stood to leave. "Crystal."

Chapter Two

“**MAT,** not that I don’t love having you here, but are you sure? This is a big gamble. Maybe you should just keep your flight home and plan to come back in a few months when Duarte and I have the orchard up and running.”

Mateus kissed his sister-in-law’s cheek and ran a hand over the slight swell of her belly. “You don’t have a few months, *irmãzinha*,” he teased.

She swatted at him. “Four months along and you and Duarte treat me like I’m made of glass. I’m perfectly capable of working in the orchard, thank you.”

Mateus pursed his lips and tried to choose his words carefully. He was on dangerous ground here, and though his English was fluent, it could be a little abrupt at times. He had to be careful of the cultural divide between them too. The machismo gallantry that had been bred hard into him by his parents back in Portugal was thought of negatively here. Bree had called it patriarchal fuckery in a screaming argument a few weeks ago when he'd said he wasn't sure if she should be driving in her condition. The memory still made him smile.

He'd been referring to her badly stubbed toe and the broken flip-flops (another fabulous word he'd learned) she'd just tripped over, but after the scolding he'd gotten, he'd been too cowed to point that out.

He decided to go with the truth because Bree had an excellent bullshit meter. "I don't like the thought of you bending and stooping to trim trees in a few months is all. Besides, which of us is the botanist, eh?"

She wrinkled her nose but didn't argue. They both knew her strength was bookkeeping. Even Duarte was in over his head with the orchard itself. It's why Mateus had come over from Portugal three months ago.

He hadn't expected to fall utterly in love with the Pacific Northwest. He knew he could make the small orchard flourish if given enough time, but his visa would run out next week.

"I don't want you to get in trouble," Bree said finally. "What if you cash in your return ticket and this scheme of yours doesn't work? What then? A one-way ticket to Lisbon will be twice what you're getting back."

That was true, but Mateus had scoured the Internet looking for ways to stay in the country. A work visa was his best bet, but the orchard had to be financially solvent to make that an option. And it would be in a few months. So all he had to do was cross the border into Canada and have his passport stamped, and his automatic American visa would re-up for another three months as soon as he landed back in Washington. It was foolproof.

The only problem was he needed the money from his return ticket to Lisbon to pay for his round-trip fare to Vancouver.

"You worry too much," he said, waving off her concern. "The tourist visa is a formality. A lot of people have done this. It will be fine."

He hoped it would be. The only other option was for him to go back to his tiny apartment and the boring, dead-end job he'd taken a sabbatical from to come here. That was the last thing he wanted now that Duarte had married Bree and the two of them had settled in the States. He'd hoped maybe Bree would want to come to Portugal, and Duarte would decide to run the olive grove their parents had left them, but Bree had a large family she couldn't imagine leaving. And all Duarte had in Portugal was Mateus and a tiny stand of olive trees that barely made enough money each year to pay the taxes on the land.

Mateus hadn't begrudged Duarte his chance at happiness in the States. He wanted the best for his brother, and Bree was exactly that. And when that little family expanded to include one more in five months, Mateus wanted to be there. He didn't want to be an uncle in name only—he wanted to be involved, just like he wanted to be involved in the orchard. This was his life now, and all he needed was a green card to solidify it.

Bree reached out and tucked her arm around his waist. "You've already done so much for us. Are you sure you want to stay? Really want to? That you're not just doing this for us?"

He wrapped an arm around her shoulders as they started walking toward the house. The whitewashed clapboard seemed to glow in the light of the setting sun, and between that and the faint reflection of the pink-streaked sky in the windows, the sight was breathtaking. The house was the only part of the orchard that hadn't fallen into disrepair under the old owners. It might take a few years to bring the trees back to their former glory, but he'd get them there. But neither he nor Duarte had an ounce of home-repair talent, so it was a mercy that the house had been so well-kept.

"I'm maybe doing it a little bit for you," he admitted. "But a lot for myself. I want a life like the one you and Duarte are building here."

She snorted. "A wife and a baby? Now I know you're lying."

He laughed and bumped his hip against hers. "Well, not exactly what you have here. But a charming home? Soil I can sink my hands into and land I can make something of? Yes."

"And maybe someday a husband and a baby?" she asked, her tone probing.

It wasn't like they hadn't talked about this before. He was ready to settle down. He wanted to—he'd just never found the right man. His parents had been far from perfect, but they'd had a wonderful marriage. And Duarte had forged the same strong bond with Bree. How could he settle for anything less than true love after seeing how happy it had made them?

"Maybe someday, if it's meant to be. You can't rush fate."

Bree shook her head. "Duarte says the same thing."

"Our *avó* Margarida used to tell us that. Mostly when we complained about things we wanted that we couldn't afford."

"Ah, your infamous grandmother. Is she also the one who I can thank for that stinker Duarte likes to pull out about the man being the breadwinner and the woman being the bread baker?"

Mateus huffed out a laugh. He doubted that. Their avó hadn't been the kind of obedient wife who would wait at home by the hearth, so Duarte had taken a lot of artistic license if he'd attributed that to her.

"I think she'd have clocked Duarte over the head with the nearest bread pan she could get her hands on if he'd used that line on her." He shot her a sidelong glance. "And apologies, but you'd be a terrible baker."

Bree burned just about anything she touched, so the kitchen was firmly Duarte's domain. But Mateus understood what his brother had meant. They were both worried about Bree overexerting herself. She seemed hell-bent on proving that pregnancy wasn't a debilitating condition, and Mateus knew she was right. But he also knew that she tired much easier than she used to. He shifted so she could lean against him as they meandered, and she sighed but didn't fight the extra help. She must be exhausted if she wasn't brushing him off.

"I'd have hit him, but I don't want to teach the baby that violence is the answer," she said mournfully. "And I think he was talking about metaphorical bread anyway." She nodded toward her stomach. "You know, a different kind of oven."

"I've never understood that analogy," Mateus said, following her gaze to the bump she now rested a hand on.

"Most analogies don't make much sense. I mean, who decided to call biceps guns?" They'd reached the porch, and she stepped away from his light embrace and sank down onto the swing he and Duarte had repainted a cheery yellow last month. "Guns are weapons. They're used to intimidate and influence people, and they can kill. If any body part should be called a gun, shouldn't it be breasts?"

Mateus might not be sexually attracted to women, but he could appreciate a nice set of breasts. And Bree's definitely were that. Pregnancy had made them a little fuller, though he'd only noticed that after she'd complained about it.

"Do you intimidate many people with your guns, then?" he asked, amused.

She gave them a little shake, then winced and folded her arms across her chest protectively. "Ouch. It's like having a perpetual case of PMS," she muttered.

He laughed and flexed his bicep. He'd always been a runner and he enjoyed playing sports, but these last few months of manual labor around the orchard had packed on more muscle than he'd ever had before. "Your guns are prettier," he conceded.

She giggled herself into a fit of hiccups that left her holding her belly, which was how Duarte found them.

"Are you harassing my wife again, *maninho*?"

Mateus grinned at him. With Bree and Duarte there, the orchard already felt more like home than Portugal. Now he just had to find a way to stay. "Always."

Chapter Three

“**NOT** the black one. It makes you look like a funeral director.”

Crawford huffed but put the suit back in the closet. “Funeral directors don’t wear Calvin Klein.”

His nephew stuck his tongue out. “Says you.”

Crawford pointed a hanger at him. “Don’t even pretend you’re not going to let yourself back in here next week and borrow it for your homecoming dance. You’re footing the dry cleaning bill, bud. Do *not* put it back in my closet dirty.”

Brandon rolled his eyes, but Crawford noted the distinct lack of protest. Hard to believe his nephew was big enough to borrow Crawford’s clothes. Hell, at the rate he was growing, he’d be outgrowing them soon.

"And you may not borrow my shoes. Have your dad get you a pair of Ferragamos with all the money he's saving on not buying you a new suit for the dance."

Crawford's brother Adam could more than afford the shoes and the suit, but Brandon had an independent streak a mile wide. It had gotten worse once he'd turned fifteen. Lately Crawford was about the only adult he'd deign to talk to, and Crawford strongly suspected it was only because Brandon didn't really view him as responsible enough to be a real adult.

That could have a lot to do with the living room full of gaming equipment or the pantry full of sugary cereals. Though to be fair, neither of those were for Crawford. Brandon's mom had been deployed overseas around the same time Davis had left Crawford, and Crawford had thrown himself into being the absolute best uncle possible. It had helped Adam and Brandon get through their own rough patch and had served as a decent enough distraction for Crawford too. Even if it did mean he spent obscene amounts of money at the grocery store each week so Brandon would have food to eat when he came over to spend hours playing video games. Crawford was glad he'd become a safe place for Brandon, even now that his mom was back and he didn't have to spend a few nights a week at Crawford's out of necessity.

Brandon yanked the brown socks out of Crawford's hands and tossed a pair of black ones into his suitcase instead. "How long you gonna be gone this time?"

"I'm hoping to wrap it up in a week. Two weeks tops." He poked Brandon in the stomach and grabbed the purloined socks when the ticklish teen let out a bark of surprised laughter and dropped them.

Brandon scowled when Crawford threw them into the suitcase. “Those don’t match anything.”

“They’re one of about four pairs I have that don’t have any holes in them, so they’re going.”

“I could come with you,” Brandon said. He perched on the edge of the bed, his expression guarded. “I’ve never been to Canada.”

“And unless you’ve been moonlighting as an international man of mystery, you don’t have the passport that’s required to cross the border.”

Brandon’s shoulders slumped, and Crawford kept half an eye on him as he tucked a pair of freshly shined shoes into a canvas bag so he could pack them. “Some reason you suddenly want to travel?”

“I asked Becca Johnson to the homecoming dance, and she said she’d have to get back to me, which basically means she’s using me as her backup date in case Chris Atkins doesn’t ask her,” he said with a dejected sigh.

Crawford winced. This was exactly why he’d sworn off relationships. Everyone had an agenda, and it was rarely in anyone’s best interest but their own. “Ouch. You don’t have to wait for her to make up her mind, you know. You could ask someone else.”

Brandon threw him a look that could peel paint. “And then later when he doesn’t ask her—because he *won’t*; he’s going with some upperclassman—then I’ll be the jerk. She’ll spend the dance in the bathroom crying with her friends, and no one will want to date me because I’ll come out of it looking like a dick.”

Crawford bit back a smile, knowing Brandon would see it as mocking and not amused. His nephew seemed to have things figured out pretty well for a fifteen-year-old. Hell, he had a better grasp of relationship dynamics now than Crawford had at thirty. Maybe if he’d had half of Brandon's insight, he wouldn't have fallen for a snake charmer like Davis.

"I don't know what to tell you, man. Dating sucks."

Brandon rolled his eyes. "Like I'd ask *you* for advice about dating."

Someone rapped against the doorframe, knuckles beating out a familiar refrain. Crawford and Adam had been using the same secret knock since before puberty, not that it was necessary here. No one but Adam and Brandon had a key.

"You know what they say, Bran," Adam said, quirking an eyebrow. "Those who can't do, teach."

"Harsh, Dad," Brandon said with a grin. "True, but harsh."

Crawford shook his head ruefully. "I don't know why I even try with you two."

Adam shrugged. "Because no one else would watch Beelzebub for you?"

The cat was a cranky old thing. Crawford said he was just waiting for it to die, but truth be told he loved the stupid, senile thing. "Fair enough."

Brandon dug through the clothes tossed on the bed and unearthed the old tabby. "I've got band practice all week because we're in the homecoming parade. Can we bring Bub to our house so I don't have to come over late at night? He doesn't like sleeping alone, anyway."

Beelzebub stretched and yawned at the attention, then fell back to sleep.

"Yeah, that's fine. It's probably better since I don't know when I'll be back."

Adam cleared his throat, and Brandon heaved a sigh. "Things are about to get boring," he said. He grabbed the cat. "Bub and I will be in the living room playing *Call of Duty*."

Crawford smelled a setup. He never should have told Adam that Davis would be there. He clenched his jaw and kept layering clothes into his suitcase, hoping that maybe if he didn't make eye contact with his brother, Adam would go away. Kind of like the advice his parents had always given him about panhandlers.

"It's not like you not to know when an audit will wrap up."

No such luck on the ignoring front, apparently. Crawford balled up a pair of clean boxers with more vehemence than necessary and tucked them into the collar of one of his shirts to help it keep its shape.

"It's a complicated one."

"Because of the hotel's problems or because of Davis?" Adam picked up a suit coat from the bed and turned it inside out, then tucked one sleeve into the other so it wouldn't wrinkle. At least he was a helpful meddler.

He also had a nearly perfect bullshit meter when it came to Crawford, so Crawford knew better than to try to lie. "Mostly Davis. I'm pretty sure the general manager is in over his head. From what I can tell, they're comping too many things to try to keep traffic up, and the spa is really hurting. I'll probably end up outsourcing that. Should be fairly cut-and-dried on the audit end."

Adam helped him pack in silence, which was almost worse than a barrage of questions. It meant he was trying to figure out how to say something delicately, and that was never a good thing.

"You don't have to go if you don't want to. Send someone else. You do that all the time."

Crawford blew out a breath. "Can't."

"This isn't some ploy to win Davis back, is it? Because—"

Crawford threw the bottle of shampoo in his hand at his brother, catching him square in the chest. "No! I didn't get a say in this. I told George I didn't want to go, and he said he'd fire me if I didn't."

Adam checked the cap on the shampoo and lobbed it into the open toiletry bag on the bed. "Seriously? He actually said that?"

"It was heavily implied."

"That's discrimination. I could have a brief on his desk by tomorrow morning."

Adam was speaking as a sympathetic brother, not as an attorney. Besides, Adam specialized in tax law. This was hardly his area.

Crawford couldn't help himself. The sight of his brother so obviously outraged on his behalf made him smile. He shook his head. "Thanks, but no thanks. It's really not. I have no doubt he'd do this to a heterosexual divorced couple if he thought it would help the bottom line. He's a ruthless asshole, but not a homophobic one."

Adam scowled. "You're one of the highest-ranking schmucks there, aren't you? If you say you don't want to go somewhere, you shouldn't have to go."

Crawford rolled up a T-shirt he'd stolen from Adam in college and tucked it into the suitcase before his brother could get a good look at it. It was paper thin from repeated washings and hands down the most comfortable sleep shirt he had. "I am, but unfortunately one of the few schmucks who outranks me is the one telling me I have to go." He shrugged, hoping it came off cheeky instead of defeated. "I probably could draw a line in the sand and refuse. I doubt George would *actually* fire me over it. But it would cause a lot of drama, and that's just not worth it."

"More drama than an audience with the queen himself?"

Crawford huffed humorlessly. "If Davis heard you call him a queen, he'd lay you out flat."

"If the tiara fits," Adam muttered. "Seriously, though, are you going to be okay? You haven't seen him since the divorce went through, have you?"

"No, but we've been on a few conference calls together. I can manage. I'm good at my job, Adam. You don't make it this far in the hospitality world without having a very convincing shit-eating smile."

"Kill him with kindness while you mentally plot his death?"

"More like divide the work up between us in a way that keeps us apart, and politely but studiously ignore him whenever possible." It wasn't the most mature plan, but it was all Crawford had been able to come up with.

He and Davis both had a knack for problem-solving and putting other people at ease, which were essential skills for the kind of troubleshooting jobs they often did. And George had been right when he'd said the hotel needed someone with Davis's skill set. It had a failing spa, much like the one Davis had revived in the Paris flagship hotel. It was Crawford's involvement that was less than necessary, and he fully intended to use Davis's gigantic ego to his own advantage.

Adam was less than impressed. "So you're going to let him walk all over you? How novel."

"I am going to do whatever I have to do to get through the next two weeks," Crawford said through gritted teeth.

"And if George decides to make you two a regular team? What then?"

Then he'd quit. It was something he'd daydreamed about with alarming frequency, and not just since George had dropped the Davis bomb. The truth was, Crawford hadn't been happy for a while. Maybe it was time to test the waters somewhere else. He'd love a job that gave him more face time with guests. The corporate rigmarole was tedious, and lately the payoffs just hadn't been worth it. He'd always intended to start a little inn of his own when he could afford it, and thanks to the prenup Adam had bullied him into getting when he'd married Davis, he could afford it. The only thing he'd walked away from that marriage with had been the money he'd brought into it—it certainly hadn't been his pride.

"George needs Davis in Europe, and he needs me here. This won't become a regular thing. We're both too essential to have us teaming up very often. This is just a special case, since it's Canada's flagship hotel."

Adam clucked his tongue. "One, that sounded incredibly egotistical. And two, George will do whatever's best for his bottom line, and if that's putting you two together, then he will."

Although they'd only met a handful of times, there was no love lost between Adam and George. He was convinced George was taking advantage of Crawford, and lately Crawford was inclined to agree. It felt more like he was working just for George instead of the company, but the only recourse he had was going to the board, and that wasn't something Crawford wanted to get into. He hated confrontation, which was a strange thing to dislike for someone who'd chosen mediation and management auditing as a career, but there it was. He was great at advocating for the company or their customers, just not great at advocating for himself.

"You need a new job. My firm—"

Crawford cut his brother off with a sour look. Adam had been trying to get him to make the change to law for years, but it wasn't something that interested him. He was a licensed mediator, but that wasn't the part of his job he really enjoyed. He much preferred working with people before things got to the point where legal action was being threatened. The conflict thing again.

"Okay, fine. But there are firms out there where you'd fit in well, you know. Hell, if you really want to help people, go back and get your masters in social work. God knows the state could use some people with good heads on their shoulders."

That didn't appeal either, though it was closer to what he wanted to do than working in some stuffy law firm. "I don't want to go back to school. I want to finish packing so I can get to bed at a decent time because my flight leaves at ridiculous o'clock, and I'd like to at least be well rested as I head into hell."

"At least think about it," Adam said, holding up his hands. "Maybe not social work, but what about another hotel chain? Couldn't you do what you do somewhere else?"

Crawford raised an eyebrow. "Looking to get rid of me?"

Adam sighed. "This wasn't how I wanted to tell you, but yeah, kind of. Karen is getting a promotion. They're moving her to Okinawa, and Brandon and I are going with her."

Crawford swallowed thickly. Moving? They were the only people in Los Angeles that Crawford cared anything about. Hell, he'd taken the promotion to the corporate office mostly because it meant he'd get to live near them. Crawford had never had many friends outside of work, and the divorce had alienated him from most of them. If Karen moved and took Brandon and Adam with her when she deployed, he'd literally have nothing left here.

"That's—" Crawford groped for words and came up short. He wanted to be happy for them, and he knew he would be, later. It must be a hell of a promotion to take them to Japan, and it meant Karen was moving up the ranks like she'd always worked so hard to do. "—sudden."

Adam sighed and ran a hand through his thinning hair. The lines on his face were getting worse every year, and even though Adam jokingly called them laugh lines, Crawford knew it was the worry he felt every time Karen was deployed etched there. Crawford hoped this promotion meant Karen would be in a more administrative role and not shipping out every few months for somewhere dangerous where Adam and Brandon couldn't follow.

"It's not that sudden. She's been up for one for a few years, but they finally got their heads out of their asses and promoted her. I'm leaving my firm, but there's a job waiting for me in Okinawa. And there's a great school for Brandon."

God. Here he was thinking about how terrible this was for him; meanwhile Brandon was going to have to be uprooted from all his friends and plopped down in a high school with a bunch of strangers. *Way to be selfish, Crawford.* "Does he know?"

"Yeah. I asked him not to tell you yet. He's pretty excited, actually. He knows a few kids there already, I guess. He's a good egg. He doesn't really care about this girl turning him down. He's just being dramatic." Adam rolled his eyes. "I wonder who he gets that from?"

Crawford's chest was heavy, but he smiled anyway and took the bait. "Surely you're not referring to me? I'm hardly what anyone would call a drama queen."

Adam tossed a balled-up shirt at him. "You may not be the queen, but you're definitely in the court."

The tight ball in Crawford's chest eased a little at the familiar jab. Things didn't have to change because Adam was moving. And it wouldn't be forever. No one in the Navy ever stayed in Japan after retirement, did they? They'd be back. Probably in a few years. It wasn't the end of the world. Besides, he'd always wanted to visit Japan. Chatham-Thompson didn't have any properties there, so he'd never been, despite his globe-trotting job.

"You've always been the one taken to flights of fancy and dramatics, not me," he said.

Adam grinned. "You're the one who decided Aunt Edna was a zombie when you were six."

"Her skin was always cold, and she smelled like death!"

"She smelled like Bengay."

"Same difference." Crawford dropped what he'd been holding and hauled Adam in for a hug. "I'm happy for you. You're happy, right? You seem happy."

Adam's face lit up. "I am. I'm just so damn relieved she's heading somewhere we can go with her. You have no idea how hard it is to be left behind like that."

Crawford's smile went tight, and Adam immediately backpedaled. "I mean—"

"No, you're right. I don't. It must be so hard for you and Brandon knowing she's in danger all the time. I don't know how you two do it. You're awesome. I couldn't do what you do. I can't imagine."

Adam looked stricken. "I didn't mean it like that."

Crawford gave his brother another hug and released him. "No, I know. I know. But Davis leaving me isn't even in the same realm as what you guys go through every time Karen ships out. I'm glad you get to go with her this time."

He shot Adam a look, hoping it came off as playful and not wounded, since he still felt pretty raw. Not that he wanted Adam to know that. "I mean, unless she tells you sometime in the next week or so that she doesn't want you to come because she's tired of you and you've served your purpose. And then starts dating someone half your age when she gets to Okinawa. If *that* happens, then yes. I'll know exactly what you're feeling."

Adam snorted out a laugh. "You're awful. And I'm sorry."

"Nothing to apologize for. And I am a little awful. It's what makes life fun." And it would be all he had to make life fun once Adam left. "When are you moving?"

"Three weeks. I had epic plans for us, you know. But then you had to go and ruin it by going to Canada."

Crawford pursed his lips. "If I had to guess, I'd say your epic plans involved me helping you pack, so I'll pass. And since I doubt you even had plans for *that* before you found out Davis would be in Vancouver, I'm calling bullshit on the whole thing. You can't get me to stay by trying to make me feel guilty. It's my job, Adam. And I'm good at it. And so is he, even though I'd much rather he was awful at it. He's a prick, but he's got good instincts and people skills."

Adam growled. "My ass."

"He was pretty good at that too," Crawford said, managing to curl in protectively around himself before

Adam pounced a second later and hit him with a light uppercut to the ribs. Hard enough to hitch his breath but probably not hard enough to bruise.

"Uncalled for," Crawford said after his coughing fit subsided and he had his breath back.

"Ditto," Adam said, still scowling. "I'm going to miss you."

"Pffft. We'll talk all the time. You're not getting rid of me that easily. And if you think I'm missing the opportunity to have a free place to crash in Japan, you're crazy."

Brandon popped his head in the door. "Are you done, or are you still hugging it out? Is it safe? I don't want to get caught in the cross fire."

Adam and Crawford looked at each other and nodded. Brandon had about a two-second head start as he read their intentions and peeled off toward the living room, but he wouldn't get far.

"Hug sandwich?" Adam asked, his eyes sparkling.

"Obviously."

Chapter Four

MATEUS loved to fly. When he'd been a child, his father had taken him up often in his tiny Cessna so they could monitor the sprawling fields that had been in their family for generations. By the time he was six, Mateus could identify ripened olives from the air. By the time he was nine, he could competently pilot the plane himself, under his father's watchful eyes.

Mateus shifted in the uncomfortable airport chair, antsy to board. He should have taken this flight a few weeks ago, but there had been a late frost and he'd had to help Duarte and Bree cover all the buds. On top of the hard winter they'd had and the late spring, they could have lost the entire crop of apples to the unseasonable cold snap.

It was fine. Sure, he was out of money. He'd cashed in his return ticket to Portugal to get the money for the round-trip flight to Vancouver, and it had left him little wiggle room. But it wasn't like he had many expenses. He didn't need much, especially with Duarte and Bree providing food and shelter in exchange for his work in the orchard.

Mateus drummed his fingers against the plastic armrest, too keyed up to stay still. They'd be calling for first-class boarding any minute now, though, so he didn't have time to take a walk to burn off some of his energy. He'd feel so much better once he re-upped his visa. Duarte was sure that in ninety days he'd have the orchard's finances in good enough shape to actually pay Mateus a wage, which should be enough to get him a work visa. Mateus didn't even care how much Duarte could pay him—he just needed the steady job so he could have a reason to stay in the States.

To pass the time, Mateus let his eyes wander around the packed terminal. It was storming somewhere to the east, and that had caused a slew of delays and cancellations. He watched a harried businessman argue with an increasingly irritated desk clerk, which was more entertaining than the network news show blaring on the television above him.

The man was absolutely striking. Tall, broad-shouldered, strong-looking, with a jaw that could cut glass and apparently a tongue that could as well. While Mateus couldn't make out the words, he could tell from the tone they were sharp. Mateus didn't know what was more enjoyable—his attractiveness or the way his voice dipped low and dangerous the angrier he got. His dark hair was sprinkled with silver, just the way Mateus liked it, so aesthetics won out.

He grinned to himself and slid down in his chair, giving himself a better angle from which to view the escalating confrontation. Mateus had always been attracted to older men. They were more settled in their lifestyle and less prone to tiresome dramatics. His preferred age had always been around late thirties to early forties, and that hadn't changed as he approached that age himself. He supposed in time it would be *younger* men who held his fancy, if his taste stayed the same.

More than just age, though, he was attracted to men who exuded a certain confidence, both in bed and out of it.

The man with the salt-and-pepper hair at the counter definitely had that going for him. He cut a fine form in his tailored suit, but it was the crisp authority in his tone that really did it for Mateus. He needed to shut that line of thinking down before he ensured a very uncomfortable flight for himself.

Mateus reluctantly tore his attention away from the scene. He had a few books in the bag at his feet, but nothing that caught his interest at the moment. He'd meant to bring the latest issue of *Annals of Botany*, but he'd forgotten in the rush of packing.

Maybe he could find a job in biotech if the orchard stayed unprofitable, he mused. Lab work had never really appealed to him, but those types of firms had big allotments for work visas. It might be a way to keep himself here, and it would only be a few years' commitment. By then surely he and Duarte would have the orchard back to full productivity.

It was all just bad timing. The run-down orchard hadn't been a bad buy. Duarte had the expertise to bring it back to life, especially with Mateus's help. The loans

Duarte had taken out to buy it had been a safe bet, but the economy had taken a dive shortly afterward, sending the variable rate interest loan that had seemed like a good deal at the time sky-high.

Throw in a bad growing season or two and it was a recipe for disaster. His brother had been forced to begin selling off parcels of land to keep up with the payments on the mortgages, but he was down to the orchard itself now, so that avenue was closed off.

Shaking off those fruitless cogitations, Mateus let his gaze roam around the terminal once more, covertly eyeing the businessman he'd been watching. When his argument at the check-in counter hadn't gotten the fellow anywhere, he'd taken a seat across from Mateus. He'd had the man pegged as first class, but he hadn't disappeared into the first-class lounge after he'd finished with the clerk. He'd focused his glower on the smartphone in his hand, his jaw set in a hard line as he scrolled through something that kept his interest. The designer suit he wore couldn't hide all that coiled strength or the way each motion made his biceps bulge.

Mateus craned his neck a bit to try to read the mystery man's ticket, which was tucked into an outside pocket on his satchel. From his suit he looked more like an attaché-case type, but the bag was leather and obviously expensive. A hipster businessman, then. Mateus couldn't make out anything other than the boarding zone, which was the same as his. So coach. Huh. That was odd. The guy had first class written all over him.

It wasn't a huge surprise when the desk clerk made the announcement that their flight was delayed. The distinct lack of an airplane at the end of the Jetway was one obvious clue. And for another, no crew had shown up to board. The handsome man stood suddenly, moved his things out of the way, and pointed to his seat. His glower had been replaced with an inviting smile, and Mateus had a flash of irrational, white-hot jealousy until he realized the man was motioning to a hugely pregnant woman. She took the seat with a grateful nod, and the man was gone an instant later, gracefully navigating the slew of phone chargers, luggage, and people that littered the floor. Mateus observed him as he made his way over to the window and started pacing, his ridiculous satchel slung over his shoulder, carelessly wrinkling his suit. His wingtips were well shined, and his pants still had a crease in them, so he couldn't have traveled far to this point. Maybe he was a local.

Which reminded Mateus of his next priority after his visa mess was sorted out. He needed to get into the local dating scene. He'd been to Seattle to check out a few clubs, so it wasn't like he'd been a monk, but he wanted more than just the opportunity to scratch an itch. Maybe Bree's meddling had hit closer to home than he'd thought.

"Ladies and gentlemen, we have a gate change for Flight 892 to Vancouver. It will now be leaving out of gate B12 in terminal two. The new departure time will be two thirty. We apologize for the inconvenience."

Everyone around him rose and began stuffing things into bags with abandon. Several people took off running like they were in danger of missing the flight. Mateus glanced down at his watch, just to check. It was barely noon. People were always so high-strung in airports.

He flicked his gaze over to the well-dressed man, a little surprised to see he hadn't been one of the ones to bolt off toward the new gate. Mateus took his time packing up his things, though he didn't have much with him. He had a five-hour layover in Vancouver—well, it would be three, now—before he boarded a plane back to Seattle. He'd brought a small case with some books, his laptop, and some toiletries, along with a change of clothes just in case, and he was glad he had. With the way things were going, he was probably going to end up stuck in Vancouver for the night—once they finally got there.

Eh, there were worse ways to spend a day. Even though he didn't understand the high anxiety most travelers seemed to share, it was fun to observe. He loved sitting back and people-watching, and airports were a great place to do that. People were in short supply in the tiny town his brother had settled in. At home in Lisbon, he could waste an entire day sitting in a park or at an outdoor café, watching the people go by, easily separating out the tourists from the locals by the way they dressed and walked, and then guessing at the nationalities of the tourists. It was a fun game.

Mateus stretched and stood up, slung his messenger bag across his body, and grabbed his small rolling suitcase. There was a coffee place at the end of the concourse. He could wander that way and get a drink before hopping the tram that would take him to terminal two. Maybe he'd grab some lunch as well. It was a short flight to Vancouver, but then he'd have to go through customs, and that could take a while. His stomach growled right on cue.

So. Lunch first, then. And a coffee after. He set off through the crowd, scanning the bright neon signs along the concourse. He hated eating in airports. Not only was the food often greasy and unappealing, but all the smells mixed together. The unappetizing cacophony of scents usually gave him a headache, and today was no different. His temples pulsed, and he rubbed a hand across his forehead, trying to dispel the tension there. Something simple and then coffee.

He'd never had lettuce in an airport that didn't end up being slimy and gross, so he passed up the boxed salads and picked up a container of yogurt topped with granola and fruit. It would ease the hunger enough for him to take something for his headache, and he could get something more substantial in Vancouver. Or maybe actually leave the airport and get some real food if his flight ended up being delayed too badly on the way back.

There weren't any free tables at the food court, which was probably a blessing. He needed to get away from the food smell before his headache ramped up and he ended up nauseated too. He slipped the fruit into his bag and made sure the top on the yogurt was tight before striding off toward the other end of the concourse, where the tram for terminal two picked up. Every gate seemed to be overflowing with passengers, so it wasn't just theirs that was delayed. The weather seemed okay, but you could never tell here. It could be fine one minute and pouring the next. That had been an adjustment—he was used to living near the coast, but this one was far less temperate. Sun was a rare commodity, and cool weather seemed to prevail all year round. It wasn't unpleasant, but he could see why some people didn't favor the Pacific Northwest.

He found a spot near a bank of old-school pay phones. The phones had been taken out, leaving only the steel frames behind. He slid into a chair and rested for a minute, trying to force his muscles to unclench. Maybe terminal two had one of those pay-by-the-minute massage places. He rolled his shoulders, wondering if he was tense enough to be that desperate. Probably not.

He should have eaten more for breakfast, but he'd hoped to be in Vancouver by now. He opened up his yogurt, figuring he could take his fruit on the plane for later. He was too worried about the yogurt going bad to risk waiting to eat that. Though if it had been the tangy, tart kind of yogurt he'd grown up with, there probably would have been enough good bacteria in there to ward off anything nasty. He still hadn't quite gotten used to the sweet, thick yogurt Americans favored. It would do for now, though, and it was worlds above the greasy burgers or soggy pizza offered elsewhere.

He dug a spoon out of his bag and forced himself to take a bite. It wasn't terrible, but the granola was soggy from sitting on top of the yogurt. He stirred it in and decided to just bolt the entire thing down. It would take his stomach a few minutes to register that he wasn't still hungry, but at this point it was more about getting it down than actually enjoying the food.

As he was swallowing a particularly big bite, he saw the handsome businessman walk by. He'd pegged him as a health nut from his rangy muscles and his overall clean-cut aura, but the man had a bag from McDonald's in one hand and a bag of Auntie Anne's pretzels in the other. So he'd clearly misjudged that one.

Mateus knew he shouldn't say anything, but he was too intrigued not to. "Looking for a spot to sit? Not a lot of competition for these old phones, so you're welcome to join me here."

The man looked startled, but after a slight hesitation walked over and sat a seat away. "You're headed to Vancouver too, aren't you? I thought I saw you at the gate."

Mateus tried not to preen at that. The gate had been packed, so it had to mean something that the man had picked him out of the crowd. "I don't think there's a very good chance the plane will be there when we get over to terminal two," he confided.

"No, definitely not. There's a mechanical problem, and they said they were flying in a part from somewhere else. That's why we're changing gates. It's closer to where the other plane is coming in. I tried to get onto another flight to Vancouver, but they were all overbooked."

So that's what the man had been so upset about with the gate clerk. It made Mateus oddly happy to know the fellow hadn't been arguing over belonging in first class or something. He'd hate for someone so attractive to be an asshole.

"No luck?"

The man shook his head. "I'm fifth on standby on the last flight out tonight, but everything between now and then is overbooked, so there's no chance."

Mateus nodded sympathetically. "Is Vancouver home?"

He was probably trying to get back to a wife and kids. Mateus risked a quick look at the man's ring finger, but it was bare. Not that that meant anything. Many men didn't wear their rings. Even Duarte didn't a lot of the time, though more for practical reasons. With all the labor out in the orchards, a ring could be a liability. A hired hand on the olive farm had lost a finger when his ring had gotten caught in a harvesting machine, and it had left a lasting impression on Duarte and Mateus both.

The man grimaced and shook his head. "No, I'm heading there for work."

Mateus grinned. “Not many people would be in such a hurry to get to work.”

The man barked out a laugh. “I’m not so much in a hurry to start the work as I am in a hurry to finish it,” he said. He put his bags down on the seat between them and held out his hand. “I’m being terribly rude. I’m Crawford.”

After wiping his hands on his pants in case there was any yogurt on them, Mateus took Crawford’s hand. Crawford’s grip was firm and his skin was soft and warm. Mateus knew his own callused hands must feel rough and hard to Crawford, but Crawford didn’t recoil. If anything, he left their hands entwined just a beat too long, which was interesting.

“Mateus.”

“Nice to meet you, Mateus. Wish it was under better circumstances. Though this is hardly bad for the airport, is it? I mean, my first flight got out on time, which could have been an omen of worse to come.”

Mateus laughed. “This is my only leg, so we’ll blame the delay on you, then.”

The skin at the corners of Crawford’s eyes crinkled when he smiled, and Mateus liked it more than he wanted to admit. “So where are you from, if it’s not here?” he asked, afraid that if he didn’t keep the conversation moving, Crawford would pick up his lunch and move on.

“Los Angeles,” Crawford said. His McDonald’s bag rustled when he opened it, and Mateus was surprised to see him pull out a yogurt that didn’t look that different from his own, instead of the greasy burger he’d been expecting. Crawford seemed to notice Mateus’s neglected yogurt at that moment, and he toasted him with his own container. “Gotta take what you can get when it comes to airport food," he said ruefully before taking the lid off and stirring the congealed fruit into the yogurt.

Mateus picked his own spoon back up and mirrored the motion. It wasn't going to taste any better warm, so he might as well finish it.

"I'm not a fan. I hate eating fast food," Mateus admitted.

Crawford nodded and swallowed his bite. "Me too. I'm not much of a cook, but I don't like any of this," he said, gesturing toward the fast-food restaurants lining the concourse. "Though hot pretzels are my kryptonite. I rarely have them, but since today is going from bad to worse, I decided to treat myself."

He looked both ashamed and defiant, and it was endearing. It made Crawford look ten years younger. Not that Mateus knew how old he was, but he was guessing fortysomething. The silvering at Crawford's temples and the laugh lines were a clear giveaway, though he was fit and healthy-looking.

"I've never had them, so I won't judge you," Mateus said. He looked at Crawford out of the corner of his eye, not sure if they were flirting or not. It felt like they were. Were they? Or was Crawford just happy to find someone to talk to in a boring airport during a long layover?

"What? Seriously? You've never had a hot pretzel?" Crawford's eyes widened incredulously. "Where are you *from*? Mars?"

Mateus snickered. "Portugal. We don't have—" He squinted at the bag. Grease spots were starting to soak through, and he had to fight not to grimace. "—Auntie Anne's."

"Oh, this is just one type. I mean, don't get me wrong, it's the best type. I think they dip them in butter after they cook them or something. But you can get hot pretzels everywhere. Sporting events, skating rinks, library food courts. You've really never had one?"

Crawford reached into the white bag and pulled out a small doughy nugget that was covered in large pellets of salt. It didn't look like any pretzel Mateus had ever seen, though he'd never seen any that weren't small and hard, so who knew?

"Shouldn't it be folded?"

Crawford's brows drew together for a moment, and then his expression cleared. "Oh, these are pretzel bites. But yeah, they sell the big pretzels too. These are just cut up so they're easier to eat. Less messy."

The whole thing glistened with butter, so Mateus very much doubted it was actually less messy than its larger cousin. His gaze traveled up to Crawford's mouth, drawn to the full, rosy lips. There was a tiny bit of yogurt in the corner of his mouth, and the resulting mental image made Mateus shift slightly in his seat. Bree was right. He needed to settle down and stop fantasizing about handsome strangers in airports. Well, that last bit was his own addition, but it still stood.

"You should try it," Crawford said. He held the pretzel out to Mateus.

Mateus shook his head. "They're your favorite. You keep it."

Crawford held his gaze for a second and then shrugged. He popped the pretzel in his mouth, his eyes fluttering shut for a moment as he chewed. He had long lashes, Mateus noticed. And he made eating a pretzel look orgasmic. They *had* to be flirting. There was no way this wasn't flirting.

"Your loss," Crawford said when he'd swallowed and opened his eyes again. "But they're about a hundred times better than they look, I promise. Are you sure you don't want to try one?"

Mateus's attention was now fixed on Crawford's lower lip, which was glossy with butter from the pretzel. He swallowed hard. "A small one," he said, his voice huskier than it had been only a moment ago.

Crawford grinned. He took another pretzel out of the bag, but instead of holding it out to Mateus, he let it hover between them, his expression questioning. A beat later Mateus leaned forward and opened his mouth, praying he wasn't reading this wrong. Crawford's smile grew, and he gently placed the pretzel into Mateus's mouth.

The taste of salt exploded across Mateus's tongue, followed by butter and the sweet, yeasty flavor of the dough. He'd been skeptical, but Crawford was right. The pretzel was delicious. Or maybe it was just that all of Mateus's senses felt heightened as he sat there eating out of a total stranger's hand.

The PA system blared out a page for passengers on a flight to Hawaii, and the world seemed to rush back into focus. Mateus had been so caught up in his exchange with Crawford that he'd almost forgotten they were in a busy airport. Crawford's face was dusted with a rosy blush, so Mateus guessed he'd just had the same realization. Right. It definitely had been flirting.

Mateus bit his lip to keep himself from laughing out loud. It had been too long since he'd let go and had fun with someone. He felt more relaxed than he had in weeks. Even his headache was gone, he realized. Flirting with an attractive man apparently was the cure for everything that ailed him.

"Should we head over to the new terminal?" Crawford asked. "I don't want to be late on the off chance the plane is actually there waiting for us."

Mateus stared at Crawford for a beat longer and then blinked. "Definitely."

He rose, his half-eaten yogurt still in his hand. "I was going to stop for coffee on the way. Would you like to join me?"

Crawford offered him a smile that made Mateus's pulse quicken.

"Sure. There was a chocolate shop a little farther down. I know it's not Starbucks, but I bet they have a killer mocha."

That sounded disgusting, but he'd choke down whatever he needed to if it meant spending more time with Crawford.

"Sounds good."

Chapter Five

THEY made it to the gate with three minutes to spare before their new assigned boarding time, but there wasn't a plane outside the window. Crawford was relieved. He was enjoying his conversation with Mateus, who, in addition to having a delicious accent, was also gorgeous. Crawford's usual type was blond and waifish, and Mateus was neither, which might've been part of his appeal. His patrician nose and full lips were framed by messy dark locks that Crawford's fingers itched to sweep back behind Mateus's ear.

Crawford had been in such a foul mood an hour ago, but now he was dreading actually getting on the plane and leaving. Maybe they'd be delayed a few more hours. He wouldn't mind that, and he didn't have any meetings scheduled until tomorrow morning anyway. Flying in tonight had probably been a bad idea—not that he'd been the one to book the flight. Usually he'd come in the evening before and have dinner with the people he'd be working with to break the ice. No doubt there was a reservation at a nice restaurant within walking distance of the hotel for tonight, though it would involve Davis. So perhaps the flight delays were for the best. Just as long as he was there by tomorrow morning.

He and Mateus had been chatting for the last hour, but he hadn't learned much about him, aside from his woeful ignorance about pretzels and his stance on mochas and airport food courts—neither of which he looked favorably on.

Foam from his own drink had slopped over onto his knuckles as the two of them hurried toward their new gate, and he licked at it absently. He'd gone for the mocha, while Mateus had grumbled about ruining good coffee and gotten an Americano. Sweet coffee was for mornings or late at night. It had no place in the middle of the day, and he'd told Crawford as much.

"I haven't asked—why are you going to Vancouver?"

No immediate answer came. Mateus seemed distracted by Crawford's hands. It took him a minute to register that Mateus's gaze was locked on the skin Crawford had just licked. Interesting. "Mateus?"

Mateus flushed, his sun-kissed skin turning a charming pink along his cheekbones. "What?"

"What's in Vancouver for you?"

"Ah. Nothing but a flight back, actually. I'm on a tourist visa visiting my brother, but it expires in a few days. I have to go across a border to reset it; Vancouver seemed like the easiest place to fly to do that."

Crawford hadn't realized visas were that simple. "I see. So you're here a little bit longer? And then—what? Going back to Portugal?"

Mateus's cheeks dimpled when he smiled. God, could he be more adorable? "God willing, no. My brother and his wife have an orchard, and I've been here helping them with it. I'd like to stay here permanently so I can be close to them." His dimples deepened, and he leaned in, whispering. "I'm going to be an uncle in a few months, and I want to be here for the baby."

This man was a wet dream. Handsome, with a sexy-as-hell accent, and he liked children? Crawford's heart thumped with something a little different from the physical desire he'd contented himself with over the past few years. Mateus was a dangerous man if he could awaken something other than simple lust in Crawford.

"I wish you well with that, then. So you're not even spending the night in Vancouver?"

What the hell was he doing? Mateus wasn't the kind of guy he could have a one-night stand with. Mateus seemed more like the kind of man who expected feelings and relationships—things that Crawford didn't do anymore. Things that he didn't *want* to do. Or that he wouldn't want to do, if he could step back long enough to start thinking with his head instead of his dick.

Mateus's eyes sparkled, clearly returning the interest. Crawford thought back over what he'd said, embarrassment washing over him when he realized it had sounded like he'd inadvertently propositioned him. "Shit. I didn't mean—so you're just flying back? I'm sorry you're not going to get to see any of the city."

"I'm sure I'll get back up there eventually. Sitting in the airport today is the first real sightseeing I've gotten to do. I haven't seen much of Seattle, and I hear it's a wonderful city."

"Oh, it is. It's one of my favorites. That and Portland. Everything up here is so much greener and nicer than down in LA. Though I suppose that could be said of a lot of places," Crawford said, aware he was babbling now but unable to stop himself.

"The orchard is about two hours outside Seattle. It's incredibly… what's the word?" He pursed his lips, his expression thoughtful. "Lush."

Crawford swallowed. Mateus's English was practically better than his, so he didn't for one moment believe Mateus truly had been struggling for the word. He had to know exactly how attractive he looked when he made that face, and how irresistible he sounded when his accent thickened. But unlike so many other guys Crawford had been with since his split with Davis, Mateus didn't seem to be playing a game. He just *was* that sexy, and even though he was using it to his advantage, it wasn't an act.

A sudden flurry of activity up at the podium drew Crawford's attention, and a moment later the clerk spoke into a microphone. "Due to unforeseen maintenance circumstances, Flight 892 has been canceled. We apologize for the inconvenience, but your safety is our top priority. Please head to terminal three, where we have customer-service representatives available to rebook you on other flights."

Crawford let his head sink back as he groaned. He'd called this a few hours ago. What a hassle.

"Wasn't terminal three where we came from?" Mateus asked, sounding amused.

"It was."

They watched as their fellow passengers scrambled back toward the tram, hell-bent on getting there first. It hardly mattered. This had happened to Crawford enough for him to know there would be precious few customer-service reps at the designated gate, and probably more than one canceled flight.

He turned toward Mateus. "They can help us at any of the airline's customer-service gates, and we're close to the departures check-in gates here. Want to follow the crowd or cut our losses and try a different gate?"

A woman with a roller bag cut off a man with a stroller, prompting him to erupt into a streak of cursing that turned heads from several gates around them. The child seemed unaffected, but the adults were acting like two-year-olds.

Mateus shot him a wary look. "Let's try the other one."

They'd be near the back of the line anyway, so even if they couldn't find another customer-service gate, they wouldn't be much the worse for wear.

"You said there weren't other open flights to Vancouver today, yes? So what will they do with us?"

Crawford shrugged. "Offer to put us up in a hotel. Or me, at least. If this is your airport, they'll probably send you home. They'll book us on other flights, either today or tomorrow probably. But it might not be a nonstop to Vancouver like this one was. Odds are they'll fly us somewhere else and then hop us over to Vancouver."

Crawford checked the signs overhead and set off in the opposite direction of the crowds. "Worst case, we have to come back through security again. Is that okay?"

Mateus nodded. "I don't think we're going anywhere anytime soon anyway."

Crawford rubbed a hand across the back of his neck. "When is your flight back, anyway?"

"Tonight, but that will be rebooked too, won't it?"

"Actually, I don't know what they'll do in that case. They may just cancel your entire ticket and have you rebook another day."

Mateus let out a groan. "I don't have another day. My visa runs out in two days, and they won't let me fly if it's expired."

Crawford looked over his shoulder, where the mob of people waiting for the tram was still visible. It would take hours to process all those people, and even if they were lucky enough to find a customer-service agent to help them at another desk, they weren't getting out of Seattle tonight.

"So this is crazy. And we just met, and you could be a serial killer for all I know. But hear me out. Vancouver's only about two and a half hours away. Three, tops. What if I rented a car and drove us there? I could drop you off at the airport in time for your flight home."

Mateus's brows rose. "Really?"

Crawford knew how ridiculous it sounded. Hell, if a stranger had offered him a ride, he'd have definitely said no. But Mateus desperately needed to get to Canada, and Crawford desperately needed not to delay the start of his meetings. They'd been getting along well enough over pretzels and coffee, and Mateus was a funny, well-spoken guy. Not to mention hot. Serial killers were never hot, were they? They were always loners with no social skills and polyester pants. Right?

Shit. Mateus was going to totally think *he* was a serial killer or a stalker. He shouldn't have offered. "Never mind, it—"

"No, I want to," Mateus said in a rush. "I mean, if you're willing to drive me. I don't have an international driver's license, so I couldn't rent a car. But if you're willing, I'll go. Do you think I could get the airline to refund that part of my ticket? Then I could pay you for half of the car."

Crawford waved off his concern. "We'll need to cancel the tickets, but don't worry about money. I'll expense the car. My company will pay for it. Don't worry about it."

Even if Chatham-Thompson didn't pick up the tab, it wasn't like a few hundred dollars was going to make much difference to him. It was certainly worth it if it got him there sooner.

"C'mon, I'll take care of the car rental while we're in line to cancel those tickets," Crawford said. He sped up, crossing through the point of no return for security and toward the check-in desks. He could see a few people in line, but there couldn't be more than two dozen in front of them. Much better odds than the hundreds over in terminal three.

Mateus hurried alongside him, picking up his bag when the roller wheels couldn't keep pace. "Do you have bags on the plane?"

"I do, but they'll take care of getting those to my hotel. Odds are, the bags will get there before we do. They're probably already on another flight to Vancouver."

Mateus shot him a look. "You seem to know a lot about this. Do your flights get canceled often?"

Crawford grinned. "Not often, no, but I travel pretty much constantly, so it does happen."

They made it to the end of the line, and from the grumbles of the people in front of them, it sounded like at least a few of them had been on their flight.

Mateus made a clucking noise. "That sounds terrible."

"Eh, I've never been too put out by a cancellation. They'll do their best to get you there eventually. There might be a delay. And I can work from just about anywhere, so a night in an airport hotel doesn't usually matter much."

"No, I mean traveling constantly. I can't imagine living that way. How do you put down roots?"

Crawford hadn't ever really thought about it that way. He'd traveled less when he'd been married, but since the divorce he'd seen no reason not to head out wherever he was needed. They were usually short trips—a few days here, a few days there. As long as he had his weekends home to help with Brandon whenever Karen was deployed, Crawford didn't really care where he was during the week.

"I'm not really one for roots," Crawford said with a shrug. "I tried it once. It didn't take."

Mateus gave him a lopsided grin. "That's called transplant shock. There are fixes for it. Most of the time when a plant doesn't root, it's because there's a deficiency in the soil. Do you not like your soil in Los Angeles, Crawford?"

That was one way to put it. "I like it well enough," he said lightly. "You seem to know a lot about plants. Did you learn so you could help your brother?"

They were inching forward slowly, and Crawford couldn't imagine what agony the other line must be. As it was, they'd be pushing it uncomfortably close to get Mateus to the Vancouver airport in time for his flight, since who knew how long the border crossing would take.

"Not exactly. I'm a botanist. Not so much an expert on apple trees, but I've had fun experimenting."

"A botanist? I don't think I've ever met a botanist. You're probably good with telling edible plants from poisonous ones, right? And figuring out how to grow things? I was just thinking about how this flight cancellation thing has the feel of a zombie apocalypse with the way people are running around and everything seems so dire. You'd be good to have around."

Crawford knew his non sequiturs were hard to follow for most people, but that's what happened when your best friend was your fifteen-year-old nephew. You tended to talk in pop culture references and not make a lot of sense. But he could kick ass at *Call of Duty* and *Mario Kart*, and thanks to the videos Brandon liked to watch, he could open a tin can with a brick if need be. It wasn't like he couldn't bring at least some skills to their zombie-fighting group.

Mateus didn't look the slightest bit alarmed at the turn the conversation had taken. "I'm not much of a fighter, I'm afraid. But I could keep us fed in the wilderness until we made it to a remote outpost to start over." He gave Crawford a friendly leer. "Though we'd have trouble restarting the population."

"But it would be fun to try," Crawford joked, internally crowing when Mateus's shoulders started to shake with laughter.

"That it would be. Fruitless, but fun."

"Is that a botany joke?"

Mateus looked puzzled for a moment, then laughed ruefully. "I wish I was clever enough for it to have been."

"You seem plenty clever to me. After all, the continued survival of our entire outpost is going to be on your shoulders."

And what wonderful shoulders they were. Broad and strong, leading to a tapered waist and long, lean legs. No, being sequestered with Mateus during a zombie apocalypse would not be a hardship.

A man at the front of the line started yelling, setting the entire crowd abuzz. It sounded like there were no more flights to Vancouver available for the day, which Crawford had called a while ago. The rental car had been a crazy, spur-of-the-moment plan, but now it seemed like it was actually their best course of action. He pulled out his phone and started looking at options.

"Do you have a preference for type of car?"

Mateus chuckled. "Other than one that will get us where we're going? No. I don't know much about cars."

Crawford was a car guy, but there was no way the company would spring for a luxury ride. Maybe he'd see what was available and splurge. Driving a sweet little sports car up the coast would go a long way to relaxing him for his impending doom tomorrow.

"Okay, so it looks like we can take the I-5 straight up to Vancouver, or we can bump over a bit and go up a coastal road. Prettier view, but it adds a little time. Not too much. I think we'd still be okay getting you to the airport in time, assuming the border isn't backed up."

Mateus pulled out his phone and checked the time. "I haven't been to the coast yet. Let's do that."

It was a nice day, especially for the Pacific Northwest. A little cool, but it always was. "I'm unilaterally deciding on a convertible, then. Or a T-top. Something where we can put the top down and enjoy the scenery."

They could blast the heat if it got cold. Crawford didn't often get the opportunity to enjoy a drive, since LA was a gridlocked concrete jungle. He loosened his tie. He almost always flew in his suit because he never knew who would be meeting him at the airport, and first impressions mattered. But if they were going to be driving for a few hours, there was no reason not to be comfortable.

"That sounds like an adventure," Mateus said. He brushed a strand of hair back from his face, and heat flashed through Crawford's chest at the thought of what he'd look like with it whipping around in the wind. It was too short to be tied back but just long enough to be a nuisance, and it was sexy as hell. Exactly the right length to really sink his fingers into, which was not something Crawford should be thinking about in the middle of a crowded airport. Or at all.

God, if they made it to Vancouver without him popping an ill-timed and embarrassing boner like a teenager, it would be a miracle.

Three people in line in front of them left in a huff, and Crawford and Mateus shuffled up. They were close enough now to eavesdrop on most of the conversations, and it didn't sound like any of them were going well.

Crawford scrolled through the cars that were available and found a BMW Roadster. It was four hundred dollars a day, plus mileage, but he was too giddy to care. He'd only need it for today—he'd be turning it in at the Vancouver airport in a few hours. So why not live a little? Every penny he could manage went into tax-sheltered investments that were building up his nest egg for the inn he wanted to buy someday, so it wasn't like he was burning money left and right.

He held the phone out to Mateus for his opinion before hitting reserve. "Eh?"

Mateus's mouth fell open. It really was a gorgeous car. Crawford mentally patted himself on the back for finding one that was so amazing.

"It can't cost that much to rent a car," Mateus said, clearly aghast.

Oh. Crawford thought his thumb had been over that part of the screen. He hadn't meant to let Mateus see the cost.

"We could get something cheaper, but I want this one," Crawford said stubbornly. He could afford it, and it wasn't like it was an everyday kind of expense. "I mean, it's an adventure, right? I usually drive a Jetta. Throw me a bone here. I want to splurge."

Mateus laughed. "It's your money. I can just think of a lot of other ways to spend it that are more fun than a car."

Crawford put a hand to his heart. "This is not a car. This is a thing of beauty and craftsmanship."

"My brother, Duarte, had a 1960s Maserati he bought off our grandfather. I never understood it because it broke down constantly and he spent more time fixing it up than driving it."

"Does he still have it?"

"Eh, no. It would have cost a fortune to ship it here from Portugal. He sold it to a collector and used the money as part of the down payment on the orchard. I think he actually cried real tears when the man picked it up."

Crawford winced in sympathy. If he'd had something that amazing, he'd probably cry if he had to sell it too. As it stood, he'd trade away his Jetta without a second thought, but that was one of the few bonuses of driving such a generic car. No emotional attachment.

He bit back a laugh. He couldn't even commit to a car these days.

They both looked up when the line shuffled forward again. Mateus was next. "So I'm definitely renting a car and driving. And I'd love to have the company if you want to come. But I'll understand if you want to catch another flight or make other plans or whatever they offer you. Don't feel obligated to go with me," Crawford said in a rush.

Mateus's lips curved into another of his gorgeous smiles. "I think we make a good team, even if there are no zombies."

Tension he hadn't realized he'd been carrying bled out of his shoulders at Mateus's easy tone. Crawford had been worried he'd come on too strong with the car thing, but it did make sense. He was going anyway, and he could probably get Mateus there faster than the airline. He kind of hoped they couldn't get Mateus on another flight tonight. It would be nice to have an excuse to be with him for a few more hours.

An agent beckoned to him, and Mateus grabbed the handle of his roller bag and stepped forward. "I'll meet you over at the end?" he asked, nodding toward a spot in the corner where they'd be out of everyone's way.

"Sure," Crawford said with a nod. "But really, if they offer you some way to get up there, you can take it, and I won't be offended."

"Will do," Mateus said. He offered Crawford a small salute and walked off toward the counter. Crawford only had to wait another minute or so before someone called him forward too.

Chapter Six

"**YOU** are enjoying this too much," Mateus said, wrapping his sweater tighter around himself.

Crawford threw his head back and laughed. "What's not to enjoy? Gorgeous scenery, beautiful car"—he looked over at Mateus and winked—"handsome man."

Mateus let out a pleased laugh. They hadn't spoken much since they'd left the airport. They were going fast enough that the wind made it hard to hear. Not to mention the fact that every time Mateus spoke, he ended up with a mouthful of hair.

Crawford had stayed on I-5 for a while and then jogged over to Chuckanut Drive, which the clerk at the rental car desk had told them was a less direct route to Vancouver but worth it for the scenic views. Mateus couldn't complain. It was so green here. He didn't know which was more impressive, the trees or the beautiful glimpses of Puget Sound.

Crawford had gotten the sporty little convertible he'd wanted despite the ridiculous price, and they were now driving it up the coast as promised. It was gorgeous, but it was also freezing. Crawford didn't seem to be affected by the wind, which was a small mercy. If Mateus had to freeze, at least he could enjoy looking at Crawford, who'd taken off his suit coat as soon as they'd gotten into the car and rolled up the sleeves of his button-down shirt. He looked absolutely edible, and if they hadn't been on a deadline, Mateus might've been tempted to persuade him to pull over and let Mateus take the rest of the suit off.

For a businessman, Crawford seemed to be in pretty good shape. His tanned forearms were nicely muscled and sprinkled with coarse hair. He must do something sporty outside in his free time.

Mateus cast a side-eyed glance at him. "Do you surf?"

Crawford looked over, confusion painted all over his face. "I don't think it's really good surfing up here—too many logs and rocks."

The coastline was littered with chunks of wood that looked bigger than buses, so Mateus didn't doubt that. "I mean at home. In Los Angeles."

"Not really. My brother does, and I go with him and my nephew sometimes, but it's not really my thing."

Mateus hadn't heard about the brother or the nephew. He wanted to ask more but didn't want to pry. Crawford's face had tightened when he'd mentioned them, so there must be a story there. They had another two hours in the car together, so he hoped he'd get it eventually. Then again, why would Crawford share such personal information with a stranger? They'd passed into heavier flirting sometime between canceling their tickets to Vancouver and picking up the rental, but it had all been in good fun. Crawford had given no indication that this was anything other than a lark for him, and even though it was obvious he thought Mateus was attractive, it was equally obvious it wasn't going to go anywhere.

"So what do you do to stay fit? You don't surf and you've said you travel a lot, so how are you in such good shape?"

"Mountain biking, if I have time. When I'm traveling for work, I usually end up in the hotel gym or out for a run around whatever town I'm in."

Mateus had always hated gyms, but he admired anyone who would put themselves through that torture on purpose. One benefit of all the manual labor at the orchard was that he rarely worked out anymore. It was a lot more fulfilling to get his weight training in by lifting barrels and trees than metal weights and barbells in a gym.

"And your job? You never said what you do."

Crawford glanced over at him again before focusing back on the road. "Boring stuff. I'm an auditor for a hotel chain."

"So you, what, count beds? What does a hotel auditor do?"

Crawford snickered. "No, though I have had to do inventories when we've closed a property and put things up for auction. Mostly I go into hotels that aren't making their numbers and figure out why. Sometimes it's just an unavoidable result of a market downturn. Sometimes it's bad management. Sometimes it's that the hotel is dated and needs a revamp, or needs to have its customer service overhauled."

"And you do these things?" That didn't sound like "boring stuff" at all.

"I get them pointed in the right direction, at least. I'll put a plan in place to get them on the right track and then set up some benchmarks they need to hit to show they're still doing well."

Mateus suspected it was a lot more than that. He'd always been a sucker for a man who spoke with authority, and it oozed off Crawford in waves. Delicious, seductive waves.

He looked out the window, focusing on the choppy water he could see each time there was enough of a break in the trees to see the coast. He needed to reel his attraction to Crawford in a bit or he'd make the rest of the drive uncomfortable for both of them.

Crawford seemed to agree, because he didn't continue the conversation. He turned up the radio instead, and Mateus settled into his seat and just enjoyed his silent company. That got old after about twenty minutes, though, which was how they found themselves discussing ridiculous things like favorite coffee chains.

"I'm just saying I don't see the appeal," Crawford said. "Canadians treat it like some sort of thing to be revered, but it seems an awful lot like Dunkin' Donuts to me, but with mediocre coffee and half-stale baked goods." He gestured with his hand to accentuate his point.

Mateus had no idea what Tim Hortons was—or Dunkin' Donuts, for that matter—but it was amusing to see Crawford riled up over something as mundane as a coffee-shop chain. He was gesturing wildly, and people in nearby cars were starting to stare.

Or they might just be staring because Crawford was smoking hot. That was a possibility. It was a big part of why Mateus couldn't take his eyes off him either.

"I don't get the American obsession with chains. My sister-in-law is the same way with Starbucks."

Crawford arched an unimpressed brow. "And you don't have chains in Lisbon?"

Mateus shrugged. "Eh, we do. But there are a lot of little cafés and restaurants. I prefer those. The atmosphere is better, and usually the food is better too."

Crawford didn't continue the conversation after that, and Mateus was starting to worry that he'd offended him. He was just about to apologize when Crawford spoke up.

"I avoid them when I can. Airports excluded, of course. We ate out a lot when I was a kid since my mom was an awful cook. Mostly chains. I was burned out on fast food by college. My brother and I probably had every McDonald's Happy Meal toy that existed in the late seventies." He looked over and grinned at Mateus. "Damn, I wish we still did. Those would probably be worth a pretty penny."

Mateus couldn't imagine a childhood that didn't include family meals at home. "My brother and I were lucky, I guess. Our mother was a wonderful cook. And our avó too." He caught Crawford's confused look. "Grandmother."

Crawford bobbed his head. "Ah. Did you grow up near your grandparents? Mine were on the other side of the country, so we didn't see them very often."

"My avó lived with us when I was a kid. Or rather, we lived with her. It was her farm, and we were her free labor." The farm was probably the reason Mateus had gone into botany. He'd loved working outside and nurturing things into bloom.

Mateus stopped himself before he could lapse into boring reminiscences, but Crawford made an interested sound and gave him an expectant look like he wanted to hear more.

"It's an olive grove. We still have it, Duarte and I. We inherited it after our parents died. It's not really big enough to make a living at it, so we lease the land to one of the neighbors. His grove is a lot bigger."

"So that's why you're in Lisbon instead of at the family farm? Do you miss it?"

Of course he did. That was a big part of the reason he'd volunteered to come help at Duarte's orchard. "I do, but it's not the same. You can't relive your childhood, you know? Some things seemed magical back then, like taking gas heaters out into the groves when the temperature dipped—I remember staying up all night as a child toting gas to the lamps and watching them, curled up on blankets out in the grove. But as an adult? All I could think about was how much the fuel cost and how uncomfortable the ground was."

He laughed ruefully, and Crawford joined in. "Yeah, I can see that."

"We haven't had to do that yet at my brother's orchard, but I'm sure we will. It seems to be cooler here than in Lisbon, and the apple trees are so delicate. He's had a hard time with them, which is why I came over to help. Plus I have him and Bree here. I was lonely at home, missing them."

Crawford cleared his throat. "I've always stayed as close as I could to my brother, Adam. He moves around a fair bit, since his wife is in the Navy, but they've been in Los Angeles for a few years. It's why I moved there, so I could help him with my nephew, Brandon, while Karen was deployed. But they're moving to Japan in a few weeks. I'm not sure what I'll do without them."

The bleakness in Crawford's voice made Mateus want to reach out and hug him, but he didn't think that would be welcomed. No matter how much of a connection Mateus felt with him, Crawford was still a total stranger. They'd been pushed together by circumstance, and that had helped them forge a bond quicker than usual. Mateus needed to keep reminding himself of that.

It was surprisingly easy to talk to Crawford. The drive flew by as they chatted, and Mateus was not at all happy to see signs announcing the border becoming more and more frequent. He was going to be sad to lose this strange bond he and Crawford shared once Crawford dropped him off at the airport.

"I'm sorry," Mateus said at last, at a loss for what else to say. He remembered how lost he'd felt when Duarte left Portugal.

Crawford shook his head a bit, as if trying to shake off the melancholia that had descended. "It's not like I won't get to see them. And it'll only be for a few years. I've always wanted to see Japan, and now I have a built-in excuse to travel there."

"I've never been, but I've heard there are a lot of chain restaurants," Mateus teased.

Crawford's laugh filled the car, and a thrill ran through Mateus at the sound. It was rich and gorgeous, and Mateus wanted to preen about being the one to coax it out of him.

"Actually, there's a chain there called Mister Donut that's really well-known. It's related to Dunkin' Donuts, like, literally. They were founded by a pair of brothers. I've always wanted to try it to see if they're alike in concept only or in taste too."

Mateus snorted. "Of course you'd travel all the way across the world for donuts. I'm not surprised, since I saw you have a religious experience with a pretzel."

He shouldn't dwell on that mental image for too long or things would get very uncomfortable in the confines of the car. Mateus flexed his hands and took a breath, willing the vision away.

"You can't compare a donut to a pretzel, Mateus. They're entirely different things."

"They're both fried dough. It's all the same."

"Heathen. They're nothing alike."

"I'm just assuming, since I've never had Dunkin' Donuts—"

Crawford sputtered. "Wait, what? You've been here for what, three months? And you haven't had Dunkin' Donuts? I'm surprised they let you stay in the country. That's criminal, Mateus."

Mateus laughed at the shaky logic. "If you say so. I could use some coffee now, no matter where it's from."

"We'll stop at Tim Hortons when we get across the border. Then you can judge its mediocrity for yourself. If you say you love it, I may never be able to talk to you again."

Mateus smiled and shook his head. Likely Crawford would never talk to him again even if he did hate the coffee shop. "You have strong feelings about coffee for a man who doesn't even drink the real stuff."

Crawford made an offended noise. "I beg your pardon," he huffed out.

"You had a hot chocolate with a shot of coffee in it," Mateus said, his nose wrinkling when he thought about the mocha monstrosity Crawford had downed at the airport. The thing had smelled like a chocolate bar.

"I was having a stressful day," Crawford said. "I usually drink plain coffee."

Mateus found that hard to believe. He didn't know Crawford well—hell, he didn't know him at all—but he pegged him as the kind of guy who had a huge sweet tooth. The coffee was pretty good proof of that. Mateus wished he'd have the chance to see if that was actually a pattern or if Crawford was telling the truth about them being a rare treat because of the delayed flight and the meetings Crawford was so reluctant to get to in Vancouver.

Since they were pulling up to the little booth at the border, Mateus decided not to challenge him on it. He already had his passport out, along with his plane ticket to prove he had travel plans back into the United States, and he handed the tidy bundle to Crawford when the guard at the gatehouse asked for them.

"Where are you headed in Canada, Mr. Hargrave?"

"Vancouver. I'll be staying at the Chatham-Thompson Lion's Gate hotel."

"Business or pleasure?"

"Business," Crawford said, and Mateus had to fight the urge to put a hand out and squeeze his thigh. He had no idea what about the trip had Crawford so bitter and resentful, but it was clear he didn't want whatever assignment he'd been given.

"I hope you'll have time to enjoy some of the sights," the man said. He handed Crawford's passport back and opened Mateus's.

"Mr. Fontes? You're a Portuguese national, sir?"

"I am. I'm in the United States on a tourist visa," he said, giving the man his best nonthreatening smile.

"Sir, are you aware your visa expires in two days?"

Mateus cleared his throat and tried to calm his racing pulse. “I am, but I’ll be back in the United States before that,” he said. “My return plane ticket is in my passport.”

The man examined it, his features tight and stern. “This ticket is for today.”

“Yes, I’m flying out tonight. It’s a quick trip.”

The guard typed something and frowned at the screen. “Is there a reason you canceled your flight into Vancouver today?”

“Uh, the airline canceled it. That’s why we’re driving.”

“I’m going to need you to pull into the station so you can speak with an immigration agent, Mr. Fontes.”

Mateus swallowed and nodded. “Sure.”

“Sir, if you’ll follow the white line and pull around, another officer will be with you in a moment and show you where you can park your car.”

Shit. What had he gotten them into? This was supposed to be easy. A rubber stamp. That’s what the Internet had said. Maybe it was different if you were driving across the border?

Crawford shot him a worried glance. “Are you sure this is okay? Do you need to go back?”

Mateus’s back prickled with cold sweat, but he smiled with as much confidence as he could muster. “I’m sure it’ll be fine. And if I end up missing my flight, I’ll just sleep at the airport and get one tomorrow morning.”

Crawford clucked his tongue. “No way. If you miss your flight I’ll get you a room at the hotel. It has a shuttle service to the airport, so you’d be able to get back easily. It would be silly for you to sleep at the airport when I have access to rooms at a four-star hotel.”

That would probably cost a pretty penny. "I'll be fine at the airport," Mateus said. "Besides, we're fine on time. I have a few hours before my flight. I'm sure we'll be out of here soon."

Another grim-faced Canadian border officer was waving them forward, and Crawford pulled up to the empty spot he pointed at. "Please exit the car and leave the keys and any baggage in it. I will escort you to the office for questioning. Your car will be x-rayed and any and all baggage may be inspected. Is the registration on the car up-to-date?"

They were going to X-ray the car? How did they even do that?

"It's a rental, so I'm assuming so. All of the paperwork is in a folder in the backseat," Crawford said. He'd been unsure a moment ago, but he was back in full businessman mode now. Even in just his shirtsleeves, he looked like someone who was in charge. "What are we being questioned about?"

"You have been flagged for suspicious behavior."

"Seriously? Because he's Portuguese?"

The officer gave Crawford a flat look. "I don't know, sir. The intake officer had reason to believe further questioning was necessary. We appreciate your cooperation." He opened the door to a small building and led them to a desk that had two uncomfortable chairs in front of it. "We will let you know when your vehicle has been cleared and released."

Crawford sighed and ran a hand through his hair, and Mateus wanted to wring his hands, but that would only make him look guiltier. "I'm sorry," he said quietly when the two of them sat down. The chairs were small and close together. Their knees bumped, but Crawford didn't move away.

"It's not your fault. I guess I should have realized the canceled flight would be a red flag. I just figured since we weren't the ones who canceled it, it would be okay."

"I don't know if it's that or my visa. I didn't mean to cause you any problem."

Crawford pursed his lips. "It's fine. I'm not in a hurry for myself, I'm just worried about you getting back home."

Mateus obviously had no sense of self-preservation, because Crawford being stupidly noble was making his heart thump harder in his chest, not his fear over what was going to happen with the immigration agent. Mateus needed to get a grip.

He handed his passport over to another bored-looking border agent. Job satisfaction seemed to be low here, not that Mateus could blame them. He wouldn't want to deal with angry people all day either.

He smiled reassuringly at the man, but it didn't have any effect.

"What is your business in Vancouver?"

To reset his tourist visa, but Mateus got the feeling that was the wrong answer. "I'm just doing a little traveling. My brother lives in Washington, and I've been visiting him. I wanted to see the area."

He had to bite his tongue to stop babbling. The agent scanned his passport and studied the screen, his face impassive.

"You can't enter Canada with only two days left on this visa."

Mateus swallowed. "I have a plane ticket back to the United States for tonight."

The man's jaw tightened as he handed Mateus's passport back to him. "I'm sorry, sir."

Mateus blew out a breath. “Okay. All right. Thank you.”

Crawford didn’t accept it so easily. “That’s ridiculous! He’s still on a valid visa.”

“For the United States, not for Canada,” the man said.

Mateus put a hand on Crawford’s arm to stop him from arguing more. He didn’t think it would do any good, and he didn’t want to get Crawford in any trouble.

“It’s fine. I can call my brother and have him come pick me up.”

Crawford’s brow crinkled. “I’m not stranding you at the border. I can take you back to Washington.”

“Just to a bus station.”

“I wouldn’t feel right leaving you like that,” Crawford protested. “I have plenty of time to get to Vancouver. Do they even have buses that could get you there?”

They probably didn’t. Mateus hadn’t seen a single bus in town. But Duarte could come get him. He’d be mad as hell, but he’d come.

Crawford turned toward the desk where the immigration officer was watching them with a solemn expression. “Are you finished with our rental car? I’ll take him back to Washington.”

“Actually, sir, he can’t enter the United States.”

What?

“He technically never left the United States,” Crawford said, his voice rising. “And his visa is still valid. So I don’t understand.”

The officer’s face softened with sympathy, which only made Mateus realize how serious the situation was. The man had been nothing but stoic since they came in. If he was feeling sorry for him, it couldn’t be good.

“Mr. Fontes cannot enter the United States because his visa is about to expire and he doesn’t have travel booked. If he attempts to enter the United States, he'll be detained and deported unless he files an appeal and it's granted."

Mateus was too shell-shocked to say anything, but luckily Crawford wasn't similarly afflicted.

"Then let's file an appeal so he can get back into the States."

"He can't file an appeal until he's in custody, sir," the officer said. He turned his gaze on Mateus, and Mateus flinched back. "You're in limbo. You can't enter Canada, and you can't enter the United States."

The gravity of the situation started to sink in, and Mateus's stomach dropped. He swallowed back the panicked tears that were threatening, his throat thick with them. "How can I be expected to make arrangements to fly back to Portugal if I can't enter either country?" he asked, trying his best to keep his voice level.

"There's really nothing anyone can do. You'll be arrested either way. It's a formality, but not one we can do anything about. Your lawyer will be able to file an appeal for you, and you'll likely have to pay a fine before you'll be allowed to board a plane back to Portugal."

He didn't have the money for a ticket to Portugal, let alone a fine. "How will I find a lawyer?"

The man looked uncomfortable. "If you don't already have one or can't make arrangements for one yourself, one will be assigned to you after you've been processed into the immigrant detention center."

Crawford wrapped a protective arm around Mateus's shoulders when he started to shake. The warmth was grounding, like Crawford might be able to physically keep him in place. "Detention center? Can't we just wait here? I can have a lawyer on the phone in under a minute. You can't arrest him just for being here."

Could he really? Or was that just a bluff? Either way, it was comforting.

"I'm sorry, sir, but Mr. Fontes has no legal claim to stay in either country. He's in violation of the terms of his visa, and he'll be arrested for it. Immigration fraud is a serious crime."

The man still seemed sympathetic, but there was a note of steel in his voice. Mateus hadn't really thought of trying to re-up his visa as fraud, but apparently the government had a different view.

Crawford's arm tightened around his shoulders, his fingers digging into Mateus's arm.

"He does have a legal right to be in this country. He's my fiancé, and I'm an American citizen."

Mateus was grateful for Crawford's tight grip, because he probably would have fallen over without it. What was Crawford doing? "I—"

Crawford squeezed him tighter, cutting him off. "Do I need to call our lawyer?" he asked the man with a pointed look.

"Sir, simply being engaged is not cause to keep Mr. Fontes in the country—"

"We were planning to get married in Vancouver. We wanted to do it in the States, but then I had to take a last-minute business trip, and we couldn't get to the courthouse before I had to leave. So we decided Mateus would come with me and we'd get married in Canada." Crawford paused and shot a quick look at Mateus before he raised his head and straightened his shoulders like he was steeling himself. "We didn't mention it because we've had one too many people lecturing us about how our relationship is unnatural. It's second nature for us to keep our relationship private."

If Mateus had been able to draw more air into his lungs, he'd have choked at Crawford's pronouncement. Thanks to Crawford's tight grip, he could barely breathe, let alone protest. That couldn't be accidental. Even in his shock over their sudden engagement, Mateus could appreciate the neat little corner Crawford had painted the guard into. There was no way he could question their story without looking homophobic. Hopefully that was something he'd want to avoid.

The officer's demeanor changed immediately. The tension that had been building in his posture relaxed, and he actually smiled. "Where in Vancouver are you getting married?"

Mateus stopped breathing altogether at the question. They'd be found out for sure, and things would be so much worse—

"The Chatham-Thompson Lion's Gate," Crawford said easily. "Well, we'll be getting married at the courthouse. But we'll be having our reception there."

The officer looked at Mateus. "Who picked out that hotel?"

Mateus opened his mouth, but Crawford beat him to it. "That's a bit of a sore subject, actually. When we found out I'd be in Vancouver for work and we wouldn't be able to get married in the States at Mateus's brother's orchard like we'd planned, Mateus started looking for chapels. He found one at this hotel, but it was already booked. I guess they fill up pretty fast during the wedding season."

Mateus didn't have to put on an act to look angry. What was Crawford *doing*?

“It’s a shame, because the chapel is really pretty. But there’s this gorgeous little courtyard, and we were able to book it for our reception. We don’t have a ton of guests, so it works. There’s ivy climbing up the stone walls, and there are a few little fountains and garden beds dotted around. We’re keeping things simple, since the courtyard is pretty enough on its own. Like a picture out of a storybook.” He squeezed Mateus again, and pressed a kiss against his temple. “But even so, I’m going to be making it up to him for a long time, I think. He really had his heart set on getting married in the orchard in Washington.”

“Well, there are always vow renewal ceremonies,” the officer said. He pulled a stamp out of a cubby in the desk and stamped something in Mateus’s passport, then typed furiously for a moment. “This will allow you entry into Canada, Mr. Fontes, but you will have to check in with the Immigration Services office with a copy of your marriage certificate within forty-eight hours of entering the country. You’ll need that to get back into the United States too.”

Mateus stared at the passport as it was handed back, dumbfounded. Crawford’s stupid ploy had actually worked.

“Please take a seat in the waiting room, and we’ll get you on your way as soon as I get word that your car has been cleared. It shouldn’t be too much longer,” the officer said. “And congratulations!”

Congratulations?

Oh, right.

They were getting married.

Shit.

Chapter Seven

CRAWFORD wasn't spontaneous. He wasn't the kind of guy who made huge decisions on a whim, and he never, ever acted without thinking.

Until he saw how panicked Mateus was at the border. Literally the only thing on Crawford's mind in that tiny office was doing whatever he could to erase the terrible tension he could feel thrumming through the other man. So he said the only thing he could think of that would give them the slightest chance of getting Mateus past the border—and then back into the United States.

And now they were going to have to get married, which wasn't a big deal. It was just a piece of paper, and since Crawford had no intention of ever marrying again, he might as well use his marital status to do a good deed and keep a nice guy in the country.

Except Mateus hadn't said a word to him in the twenty minutes since they'd left the border behind them, and Crawford was starting to get worried. They were closing in on Vancouver, but Crawford didn't want to wait until they were at the hotel to hash this out.

He glanced over at Mateus, who was still blindly staring out the windshield, a cup of Tim Hortons coffee held loosely in his hands. He'd taken a few sips of it, but it had to be cold by now. Crawford had stopped at the first one he'd seen after they'd gotten into Canada, both because he really needed some caffeine and because he'd been shaking hard enough to make driving unsafe. Mateus had stayed in the car while he'd gone in to get their drinks.

Crawford couldn't take it anymore. He pulled off at the next exit and parked in the first empty parking lot he saw. Mateus blinked and turned to face him, which was definitely progress.

"Are you all right? I know I overstepped, and I'm sorry. If you don't—we can call my brother. He really is a lawyer. He doesn't specialize in immigration law, but I'm sure he'd know who we could call. He could help us find a lawyer for you, and we could go back to the border if you want. Maybe have someone meet us there so you have representation before you get taken to the detention center. I just didn't like the thought of them hauling you away like that with no one there to help you."

Mateus's lashes fluttered against his cheek, and he blew out a breath. "That would probably be best. Marriage." He laughed humorlessly and opened his eyes. "I can't allow you to make a sacrifice like that. You don't even know me. I should have said something at the border, but I was too scared to think straight."

It was a relief to hear Mateus's voice again, even if what he was saying was ridiculous. "I have absolutely no objection to marrying you," Crawford said. He held up a hand when Mateus started to protest. "I know that sounds totally stalkerish and crazy, but hear me out. Marrying you to help you get a green card would be less of a farce than my first marriage was, trust me. I'm not the marriage type, it turns out. So why not sign a piece of paper that says I am if it means helping you?"

"You can't mean that," Mateus said, his expression incredulous. "Marriage isn't just a piece of paper. It's a partnership, and it's beautiful. I'm sorry if your experience with it wasn't, but one bad marriage doesn't mean you aren't the marrying type. You'll find someone who changes your mind, and then where are we?"

Crawford was so tired of people trying to sell him platitudes about love and marriage. It was all crap. Marriage was a business transaction, a bit of paperwork that tied two lives together for taxes and other practical reasons. Starting off a marriage with Mateus, knowing it was all a sham, would probably make theirs the most honest marriage on record. Everyone went into marriage with their own secret agendas, and this way those agendas were out in the open. It didn't count as being used if you *knew* you were being used going in.

"I won't change my mind. You don't need to worry about that. And you won't need me forever anyway. Just until you can get permanent alien status or whatever it is you need to do, right?"

Mateus made a frustrated sound. "I can't ask that of you. It's so much. It can take years for all that paperwork to go through. My brother has been married for three, and he's still not a naturalized citizen."

Crawford shrugged. "So?" He shook his head when Mateus sighed. "No, listen. I don't—I'm not being a drama queen when I say marriage is off the table for me, okay? It's not like we'd actually be tied together. Just legally. We won't live in the same place. We probably wouldn't even have to see each other again if we didn't want to, once we're officially in the States as a married couple. I'll be in LA, and you'll be in the boonies in Washington doing what you do. And if you meet someone and want to get married for real—well, we'll get a quick divorce. I'm not asking you for anything here, Mateus. I promise."

It was a serious moment, but Crawford had to fight not to snicker. Here he was, asking someone to marry him again and making promises. Putting himself smack-dab in a position he'd sworn to himself three years ago he'd never be in again. It felt right, though. Spontaneous and stupid, but right. There was just something about Mateus that was—he didn't even have words for it. Good. Innocent. Carefree. Things Crawford wished he was but knew he couldn't be. And he didn't want Mateus's spirit to be crushed by getting arrested and deported. The man was just trying to help his family, for Christ's sake. He was a *botanist*. Not some horrible threat to the country. What would deporting him accomplish?

Mateus rubbed a palm across his face. He looked a lot more exhausted than he had just an hour ago. Older too. Some of the light had already gone out of his eyes, and Crawford didn't want to be responsible for extinguishing the rest.

"If you really hate the idea, we'll go back." He pulled out his phone. "My brother's firm has a lot of connections. We'll find you someone who can help."

Mateus reached over and put his hand over Crawford's before Crawford could call. "I don't hate the idea." He shot Crawford a wry grin. "In fact, I think I would not find being married to you to be a hardship at all. But I'm getting all the benefit. You—why would you do this for a stranger?"

He wouldn't, not for just any stranger. But Mateus wasn't just anyone, and he didn't feel like a stranger. Crawford had lost most of his friends after his divorce, and he had a hard time opening up and trusting new people. But it had felt natural to tell Mateus his whole life story and offer to drive him to Canada when their flight was canceled. And then to offer to marry him when the need arose. Crawford couldn't find the words to reassure Mateus, because there weren't any words. It was completely and utterly crazy.

"It just felt like the right thing to do," Crawford blurted. He flushed. It made him sound like some sort of Dudley Do-Right, and he wasn't. He recycled, he gave to charity. He held doors open for the elderly and always returned his library books on time and in good condition. But he wasn't the kind of guy who would bend over backward to help a stranger. He'd do anything for his family, but Mateus wasn't family. He couldn't explain why he felt like he was.

Mateus studied him for a long moment and then nodded. "If we do this, you have to be able to call an end to it whenever you want. No guilt about me getting deported."

"Same. For you, I mean. You should be able to end it if you want to."

Mateus's chin came up, and some of the fire returned to his eyes. "I know you don't believe in marriage, but I do. So while we're married, I'll be faithful to our marriage.

I don't expect the same of you, but I wouldn't feel right being married to you and being with someone else."

Crawford was flabbergasted. So Mateus was offering up a vow of chastity? "I don't expect that, but I can't tell you what to do. We'll be married on paper only. Your life is yours."

And mine is mine, he thought. He was definitely not signing up for a few years of abstinence. And he wasn't going to expect any kind of intimacy from Mateus either. It would feel too much like pressing an advantage. Crawford didn't like any imbalances of power in his relationships, not even the ones that were purely physical. "I'm not going to lie, I'm attracted to you," he said bluntly. "But I won't consummate our marriage. That would feel—" He groped for a word, trying to defend himself without offending Mateus. "—wrong, somehow. Like I was trading marriage for sexual favors or something. So no sex."

Was it his imagination, or did Mateus look disappointed at that? It was a shame, because he hadn't been lying about being attracted to Mateus. He was gorgeous, funny, and smart. But he was off-limits now.

"I respect that," Mateus said solemnly.

Crawford almost wished he'd put up a fight on that front. It wouldn't have taken too much convincing that it was a bad idea. But it was a good condition. And unlike Mateus, he wasn't promising to be faithful. It wasn't like Crawford was interested in long-term relationships these days anyway. He was purely into hookups and casual flings. Mateus would be neither, and the two of them being married would make things messy and complicated.

"So are we agreed? We'll get married, file the paperwork, and you can probably fly home tomorrow."

Crawford looked at the clock on the dash. "I don't think there's any way to get all that done before your flight today. But you can stay at the hotel. It's not anywhere near capacity, so it won't be a problem to arrange for a room for tonight."

Mateus bit his lip, still looking hesitant, but he nodded. "So we do it today?"

Crawford scrolled through his phone, searching for a vital statistics office as the border officer had suggested. "We do it today."

"YOU should have let me pay for the rings," Mateus said, holding the door to the hotel lobby open for Crawford.

Crawford wouldn't have thought of that piece at all, except there had been a tiny jewelry store next to the marriage commissioner's office. There had been a set of beautiful yet simple white gold rings in the window, and on a whim Crawford had gone in and purchased them. They were nowhere near as ostentatious as the platinum and diamond rings he and Davis had exchanged, but somehow they seemed to suit him and Mateus. Crawford had forgotten what it felt like to have the weight of a ring on his finger. He'd have been lying if he said he didn't like it.

He ran his thumb over the band, a smile playing over his lips. The ceremony had taken all of five minutes, and he and Mateus had been giggling by the time they'd left the courthouse. They probably looked like any other giddy newlyweds, though their hysteria had been more of a shared "what the hell have we done" rather than excitement.

"The rings were my treat." He'd slipped in to get them while Mateus had been using the restroom at the deli next door to the commissioner's office. It had felt ridiculous and more than a little romantic, which was absurd. But marriage obviously meant something to Mateus, and Crawford had wanted to honor that at least a little bit.

"I'll take you to dinner tonight, then," Mateus said with a sharp look that made Crawford grin. They'd been married less than an hour and Mateus was already starting to henpeck. He bit back the comment, knowing it wouldn't go over well. He did have some sense of self-preservation, illegal impromptu marriage notwithstanding.

"I look forward to it," Crawford said with a bow, drawing a smile out of Mateus.

"You don't have to charm me anymore, Mr. Hargrave. I already married you," Mateus muttered.

Crawford laughed, delighted to see that some of Mateus's spunk had come back. "I really am looking forward to it, though. I'm starving."

"We can walk around and find someplace after we check in," Mateus suggested. "Unless you already have something in mind? Did you have plans already?"

He probably did, but Crawford didn't care. He was never the one who made his own eating arrangements when he was working. Whoever planned the trip usually did that, and the first night was almost always spent dining with the management staff. They'd have to take a rain check this time, though. He couldn't give Mateus a real honeymoon, but he'd at least give him a meal with his undivided attention before Mateus flew out of his life and back to Washington the next day.

The immigration office had been about to close for the day, so they'd made an appointment to see someone first thing the next morning. He had at most dinner and then breakfast tomorrow to spend in Mateus's company, and Crawford wasn't going to waste any of that time.

The hotel lobby was spotless, and as Mateus craned his neck, taking in all the sights, Crawford couldn't help but be a little bit proud. He'd had nothing to do with the design of the hotel or its impeccable upkeep, but it all fell under the umbrella of Chatham-Thompson, and he liked that Mateus seemed impressed.

If the rooms were as well-kept as the lobby, his job was going to be a lot easier than anticipated. He'd half expected to see the hotel had fallen into disrepair, as was often the case at properties that had lagging revenue. If he just had to tweak some service protocols and amenities, he might actually be out of here in less than the two weeks he'd allotted, which was a good thing. It meant less time with Davis and more time at home with Adam and Brandon before they had to leave for Japan.

God. What was Adam going to say about all this? Could he even tell him? Were lawyers bound by statutes to turn people in if they knew about illegal transactions?

No, they couldn't be. In fact, wasn't most of their business built on the fact that they didn't have to turn their clients in? Maybe he'd make Adam take him on as a client, and then they'd have attorney-client privilege. Crawford was bursting to tell him about Mateus and their adventure at the border. Adam was always the fun, spontaneous brother—it would be nice to be the one telling the shocking story for once.

A well-groomed woman in the tidy Chatham-Thompson uniform all front desk employees wore flashed him a welcoming smile when he and Mateus walked up. "Mr. Hargrave! We expected you a few hours ago, sir. We have your room ready for you."

Her gaze flicked to Mateus and down to his luggage before coming back to Crawford. "We didn't realize you'd have a guest with you, Mr. Hargrave."

"It was a bit of a last-minute decision," Crawford said, and Mateus choked on a laugh next to him.

"Very last-minute," Mateus said, and the woman practically melted at the grin he sent her.

Crawford handed over his passport, and Mateus followed suit. Even though they knew who he was, it was still hotel protocol, and he wanted to save her the hassle of having to ask him for it.

"It's no problem," she said, her dimples showing when she smiled again. "We have you in one of our one-bedroom suites. Does that suit, or shall I change your reservation to a two-bedroom?"

Before he could answer, the woman reached out to take Mateus's passport, and her eyes widened when she saw his ring. She glanced over at Crawford's and gasped audibly. "Oh, congratulations! Mr. Hargrave, I had no idea you were bringing your husband! You should have told me, we could have had a suite reserved to give you extra room."

Crawford cringed. "We don't—"

"He hadn't planned on bringing me. It was a last-minute thing," Mateus put in. "It's new. The marriage."

She lit up. "Are you here on your honeymoon?"

Crawford supposed they were, technically speaking. He looked over at Mateus with a wry grin. "Yes."

Her fingers flew over her keyboard. "The penthouse suite is open. I can't believe you're spending your honeymoon here, working!" Her hand flew up to her mouth. "I'm so sorry, sir. I just mean, it's so unexpected. Not that there's anything wrong with working on your honeymoon. Or that this is your honeymoon. Maybe you're off to another property afterward for a proper honeymoon? Not that this isn't proper—"

Mateus stepped forward and stopped her babbling by taking his passport back. "It's fine. I knew what I was getting into. You could say Crawford is married to his work. I'm a bit of an afterthought."

The woman laughed. "We're very grateful to have Mr. Hargrave working with us. Mr. Franklin has already checked in, and we're so lucky to have both of them here. I hope you'll have some time for sightseeing and, uh, other honeymoon things while you're here."

Her cheeks pinked, and Crawford flushed a bit as well. "You really don't have to give us the penthouse, Michelle," he said, reading her nametag. "In fact, I really must protest and insist you don't. It should be left open for guests."

"But you *are* guests," a familiar voice said from behind him. Crawford cringed, and then steeled himself before turning.

"Davis," he said as cordially as he could. He even managed a polite smile.

But Davis wasn't looking at him. He was staring with avid interest at Mateus and the wedding ring on his finger.

"I had no idea you were getting married," Davis said when he finally tore his eyes away and looked at Crawford. His cheek twitched, just like it always did when he was annoyed, but that was the only giveaway to show he wasn't as enthusiastically pleased as his tone suggested. Davis always had been excellent at reading situations and acting exactly as he should. "And that you were bringing your new husband along to Vancouver."

"They were just married," Michelle said helpfully.

The twitch grew more pronounced. "Is that so?" he asked, giving Crawford a speculative look. "Well, then, I must agree with Michelle. We insist you take the penthouse suite. And you'll join me for dinner tonight, won't you? I was planning to dine here at the hotel with some of the management staff, but since this is a special occasion, I think that can wait. We can have the concierge secure a reservation somewhere appropriately festive."

Crawford's mouth fell open, but before he could let loose a scathing retort—Jesus, leave it to Davis to make Crawford's remarriage all about him—Mateus spoke up.

"That is so kind of you, but I have plans for my husband tonight." Mateus's voice was like velvet, making it clear that those plans he so glibly referenced were definitely not for public consumption. He ran a proprietary hand up Crawford's back and down his arm, twining their hands together.

Davis visibly flinched, his eyes widening. "Tomorrow, then. I insist. My treat, to celebrate. It really is amazing to see Crawford married again," he said, his composure returning with his smirk. The look he gave Crawford was speculative, like he could see right through him. He'd always been a lot better at reading people than Crawford had. After all, he'd correctly sized Crawford up as a chump, hadn't he?

"Ah, I don't know if I'll be done with him by then, but I don't want to keep him from his work. I suppose I can share," Mateus purred.

Davis colored a bit at the insinuation that he was nothing but a coworker. "I do wonder why you chose to get married right now," Davis said, a gleam in his eye. "The timing is a bit curious. I mean, you hadn't said anything about your husband-to-be in any of our conference calls, and then you get married the day you're going to see me?" He turned to Mateus and lowered his voice conspiratorially. "Surely you know who I am. I can't imagine Crawford hasn't told you about me."

Crawford felt like he was in the middle of a tennis match or a particularly vicious argument on some *Real Housewives* spin-off. He knew he should intervene, but he couldn't seem to make himself speak. It would be so easy to smile and shrug Davis off, claiming they were tired and needed to get up to their room. It would be totally plausible that newlyweds would want alone time, but it was also mortifying that the clerk and the entire lobby would assume he and Mateus were going upstairs to have sex.

"Oh, he has," Mateus said, his smile still firmly in place. He squeezed Crawford's hand. "Shall we go up, *meu amor*? I am anxious to see this suite that the lovely Michelle has so kindly arranged for us, and I'd like to have a little rest before our reservations tonight."

Mateus's accent seemed to thicken as he spoke, making his voice even more seductive. It had to be on purpose, and it was certainly having the desired effect. Davis visibly recoiled, and Michelle leaned in, charmed and completely under Mateus's spell. Arousal stirred in Crawford's belly, his blood heating despite his embarrassment and anxiety.

Michelle handed them a set of key cards and a cardboard folder. "Please allow me to call for a bellhop to bring your things up," she said, her cheeks flushing as she smiled. "Your bags were delivered an hour ago, Mr. Hargrave. Room service will also be by momentarily with a bottle of champagne. We hope your stay will be pleasant."

She blinked a few times and seemed to remember that Crawford was in fact there on business. She straightened a bit and took a breath. "And Mr. Fontes, please don't hesitate to call our concierge if you need anything while Mr. Hargrave is in meetings. Vancouver is a wonderful city, and we can arrange for tours and transportation if you desire."

Mateus grinned and swept his hair out of his face. God, he was good. Crawford could practically feel the jealousy radiating off Davis. This was marvelous. He hadn't thought much about how he was going to handle snide comments about his relationships, but he'd known it would happen. Davis was a smug bastard, and he never took the high road. This was going to make things easier in a lot of ways.

And from the way Davis was silently fuming, it was going to complicate things too. Good thing Mateus would be hundreds of miles away by tomorrow afternoon. Crawford would have the benefit of his newly minted marital status to deflect any probing questions from Davis, but he wouldn't be parading Mateus in front of him.

"Oh, I doubt that will be necessary," Mateus said. He shot Crawford a sultry look and winked. "I think Crawford will keep me plenty busy."

Crawford coughed to cover a laugh and tugged on their still-joined hands. "I'm sure we'll be fine," he said to Michelle over his shoulder as he led Mateus toward the elevators. "I'll be missing breakfast tomorrow morning, Davis. I'm sure you understand. I'll see you for the morning management meeting. If there are any last-minute things that have come up, just e-mail them to me."

Mateus growled playfully. "Don't, actually. No working on our wedding night."

Crawford did laugh at that. "All right, then. I'm sure anything Davis has to tell me will keep till tomorrow anyway."

He had no doubt he'd have several tersely worded e-mails in his inbox before they even got up to the room, but the teasing was worth it for the look on Davis's face. He was absolutely livid but had to smile for appearances' sake. It was a face Crawford was unfortunately well acquainted with, since Davis had worn it for most of the public functions they'd attended together for the last few months of their marriage.

"Don't worry, I'll make sure the rest of the management knows to give you a wide berth tonight," Davis said tightly.

Shit, he hadn't thought of that. George would not take this news lightly, even though it wouldn't impact Crawford's ability to do his job at all. It wasn't like Crawford could tell him he wasn't actually on his honeymoon.

"He's all yours tomorrow," Mateus said as the gleaming brass doors opened. "But for now, say good night, Crawford," he drawled.

"Good night," Crawford said dutifully, letting Mateus pull him into the elevator car.

As soon as the doors closed, Crawford collapsed against him, both of them laughing hysterically. Crawford wouldn't put it past Davis to pull the elevator camera footage and watch their ascent, but all he'd see was the two of them wrapped around each other, giggling. Which would probably do more to sell their marriage, in fact.

Crawford put his key card in the slot and hit the button for the top floor. The elevator started to move, and Crawford took a small step away, reclaiming some of his personal space.

"You're scary good at pretending to be my adoring husband," Crawford said when he'd gotten his breath back. "Appropriately territorial and all. That was amazing."

"I didn't have to pretend to hate him. He's a jackass," Mateus growled. "I wanted to punch him."

"You aren't alone in that. My brother actually *did* punch him at a party once." It had been horrible at the time, and Crawford hadn't spoken to Adam for two weeks afterward. Now he just wished he'd listened to his brother when Adam had warned him what an ass Davis was. And that Adam had hit him harder.

The elevator opened on an elaborately decorated marble foyer. It was like a miniature atrium, and the skylight overhead cast the entire room in a rosy glow. The sun would be setting soon, and Crawford bet the view from the suite's terrace would be spectacular.

The crazy day caught up with him all at once, and Crawford nearly stumbled with the sudden slam of exhaustion. "Do you want to just have room service deliver dinner? Or did you have your heart set on going out and seeing some of Vancouver?"

Mateus had walked ahead into the room and was running his hand lightly over all the flat surfaces. The leather sofa looked buttery soft, and all the mahogany tables were so glossy they shone like mirrors. There was no harsh overhead lighting here like there would be in most of the rooms downstairs—the penthouse suite was lit by dozens of lamps, and they'd all been illuminated when they got off the elevator. Either someone had been up here before them—unlikely, given the last-minute nature of the reservation—or they were on some sort of timer. Crawford made a mental note to look into that. It was a nice touch, having them on when a guest came in, but lighting a room that was unoccupied was an expense the hotel definitely didn't need.

It all felt ridiculously romantic, especially the way the city was beginning to light up in the twilight outside. Somehow this gigantic suite felt much more intimate than the car had, and Crawford figured they were in for an awkward evening—especially since he only saw one bed through the french doors into the sleeping area. The couches here were too fancy to be pullouts, and while they looked comfortable enough for lounging, neither of them were long enough to accommodate either of their lanky frames. He could call down to the desk for a rollaway bed or even insist on being moved to a room with two beds, but that would cause all kinds of talk among the staff. He'd already sparked enough gossip by showing up married—he couldn't be an effective leader if everyone was tittering behind his back about how he and his new husband had spent their honeymoon night sleeping separately.

The elevator dinged before he could broach the delicate subject of their sleeping arrangements. The bellhop entered with their suitcases, along with someone from room service pushing a cart that had a bottle of champagne in an ice bucket and a small but impressive three-tiered cake.

"Compliments of the management," the man said as he pushed the cart in. "Congratulations on your marriage! Please let us know if there's anything else we can do to make your honeymoon memorable."

The bellhop took both suitcases into the bedroom area, then opened up the terrace doors for them. "In case you'd like to enjoy your champagne outside. The hot-tub controls are just inside the door," he said with a wink. "There's a smaller balcony in the bedroom that overlooks the courtyard. It's not quite as private, but that view is lovely as well."

Crawford wanted to cringe away in utter embarrassment, but instead he pulled out his wallet and tipped both men generously. They left after the bellhop explained how to set the elevator to Do Not Disturb, which Crawford did as soon as it closed behind them. He didn't favor floors where the elevators opened up directly into a guest's room for exactly that reason.

Mateus had pushed the cart out onto the open balcony and uncorked the champagne.

"It's beautiful out here," he said, pouring Crawford a glass. "I can't believe this is ours for the night. Would it be terrible if I admitted I really want to get in the hot tub?"

He sounded too giddy to be making a pass, so Crawford let himself relax. He didn't want Mateus to think he'd set any of this up to seduce him. He'd never take advantage of him like that. But that didn't mean they couldn't enjoy what had been given to them, he supposed.

"Let's wait till it gets full-on dark. I bet the view is even better then." He scooped a finger through the icing on the bottom tier of the cake. "I guess our wedding is official now. Cake and champagne. It's the full package."

"Don't forget the rings," Mateus said. He held up his hand and wiggled his ring finger. "I admit I took a lot of pleasure in rubbing it in Davis's face earlier. I'm sorry if I made things more difficult for you in the long run."

"You've already apologized, and I've told you it isn't necessary. I honestly wasn't sure it was possible to render Davis speechless, so I'm in your debt for that." Even though Davis probably wouldn't shut up about any of this for the rest of the trip. Still worth it, though. Just for those few moments where Davis had been completely taken aback.

Mateus took a long sip of his champagne and studied Crawford with a hard-to-read expression. Crawford tried not to fidget under the scrutiny. Professional life aside, it had been a long time since he'd actually cared what someone thought of him. He didn't like the idea that Mateus might be examining him and finding him wanting in some way.

He swallowed his stolen frosting and coughed awkwardly. "So, dinner? We can get room service back up here pretty quickly, if that's still what we want to do."

Mateus wrinkled his nose. "Would it be awful if we ordered takeout instead? I'm thinking the room service food would be fancy, and I'm not in the mood for that."

Odd words coming from a man drinking from a two-hundred-dollar bottle of champagne. Crawford decided it was probably best not to share that detail with Mateus, even though the wine was comped to the room. Mateus had been tense anytime money had come up, and Crawford didn't want to spoil the moment fighting about it.

"We're not too far from Chinatown. I'm sure some place would deliver, or we could go out, walk around." He'd been so tired on the way up, but the night air and the champagne had revived him. Add to that his desire to get out of their room for a bit. It was ridiculous, since it was just a name, but being in the honeymoon suite had made Crawford uncomfortably aware of their situation ever since they'd gotten off the elevator. They were probably the first married couple to stay there who'd just pledged *not* to have sex after making their marital vows.

Mateus tossed back the last of his champagne and put the flute on the cart. "Let's do that. I'd like a walk. I'm—" He pursed his lips, and Crawford realized it was the face he made when he was searching for the right word. "—antsy is the word, maybe? Too much sitting. I like being more active."

Crawford grinned. "My mom always called that squirrelly."

Mateus lit up. "I love that. Squirrelly," he said, the word rolling off his tongue in a way that made it sound absolutely delicious. "Squirrelly. Yes. Let's take a walk, eh?"

Crawford could do with burning off some energy himself. He looked down at his rumpled suit. He'd have to send it out to the dry cleaners this week, which was something he'd planned to do anyway, since it was a good way to evaluate the hotel's amenities. "Do you mind if I change first?"

Mateus waved his hand. "I'm in no hurry." He poured himself another glass of champagne and wandered around the small terrace off the sitting room, poking at plants and looking out over the city.

Crawford hurried into the bedroom and shut the frosted french doors behind him. He leaned his head against them for a moment, enjoying the way the glass felt cool against his skin. He hadn't really had a moment to himself since he'd left for the airport that morning, and he needed a little silence to digest everything that had happened.

He needed to call Adam and tell him about Mateus. And soon. He didn't want to go into that meeting tomorrow morning without at least having the name of an immigration attorney in Vancouver who could help them if things didn't just get rubber-stamped the way they hoped they would.

He slid his phone out of his pocket and dialed his brother, sandwiching the phone between his ear and his shoulder so he could unpack at the same time. It took five rings for him to answer, and Crawford already had his jeans and a light sweater in his hand by the time he heard Adam's voice.

"Let me guess," Adam said, his tone light and full of teasing laughter. "You've already killed Davis, and you need me to recommend a lawyer who can get you off."

Crawford chuckled darkly. "Well, you're half-right."

"Ah, seriously? You've already bludgeoned him to death? Was it his hair? His attitude sucks, but it was always that Justin Bieber hair that made me want to do him physical harm."

"Davis is alive and well, unfortunately. But I do need the name of a good lawyer up here."

Adam was quiet for a beat, and then the sound of his sigh carried across the phone. "What have you gotten yourself into now?"

Chapter Eight

MATEUS dropped down onto the couch he'd spent last night sleeping on and rubbed a hand over his face. He'd slept poorly, both because of the uncomfortable position and because he'd been hyperaware of the fact that Crawford was sleeping in the bed that was only a few feet away.

It had been bearable, but only just. And even then only because he thought he'd be flying back to the States today, putting some much-needed distance between himself and Crawford. He wanted to climb the man like a tree, which would be a terrible way to repay him for the amazing favor he'd done for Mateus. The favors he *continued* to do for Mateus. Like now, letting him stay with him for the next two weeks, since the immigration office had made it clear that Mateus had to be with his new husband when he traveled back into the United States or risk being detained by Homeland Security.

The agent at the border had mentioned something similar, but Mateus had been too panicked to really listen. Neither he nor Crawford had, apparently, since that condition had come as a surprise to both of them. Once the conditions for Mateus's entry into the US had been laid out, it made sense. Even with the marriage certificate, the border patrol would need to see that they were actually together. Mateus had never really thought about how couples proved their marriages were legitimate. He'd never really *had* to think about it, because he'd never planned to fake-marry someone to get a visa.

He shifted on the sofa and groaned. There was no way he was going to be able to spend the next two weeks on the couch. Even switching nights the way Crawford had suggested would be a major pain. And Crawford was so paranoid about the housekeeping staff finding out that they weren't sleeping together. They'd had to remove all of the bedclothes and pillows from the couch before breakfast was delivered that morning.

Mateus was not a morning person. That was not going to stand. He couldn't be folding sheets every day before he even had coffee.

Early morning paranoia aside, Crawford had been amazing. Which Mateus was beginning to think must be his default, because he'd been his knight in shining armor ever since they'd met a little less than twenty-four hours ago. Every time something unexpected and awful happened, Crawford was there to smooth it over and come up with a solution that sounded perfectly reasonable in the moment. Like getting married to keep

Mateus from getting deported. Like inviting Mateus to stay with him in his fancy hotel because the immigration office was closed for the night, and then joining him for Chinese food before staying up late eating cake and drinking flat champagne out on the terrace even though they had to be up early the next morning. He'd been totally cool and collected through everything, aside from his tendency to bite his bottom lip when he was nervous. As tells go, it was an obvious one, but since his lips were so delectable anyway, it came off as attractive. Everything about him was adorable, even his nervous tics.

Which brought them to the latest rescue. He'd chewed the hell out of his lip while absorbing the news that he was stuck with Mateus for the rest of his trip, since Mateus couldn't get back into the United States without him. If things kept going at this rate, Crawford's lip would be a bloody mess by the end of his business trip, and Mateus couldn't have that. He'd have to figure out a way to ease the tension. They hadn't had time for much discussion after the immigration officer had dropped that particular bit of news on them, since Crawford had been rushing to get to a morning meeting with Davis and the hotel management staff. He'd even had room service send lunch up when the meeting went long and he had to miss their promised lunch date.

Not that it had been a date. Though Mateus very much wished it had been. Could you date your husband? He huffed out a laugh and burrowed deeper into the couch. Maybe he'd nap. And when he woke up, he'd be back at the orchard in the sunny yellow guest room Bree had painted herself. The room that would make a perfect nursery, if only Mateus wasn't currently living in it.

He just seemed to put people out no matter where he was.

Mateus sighed and made himself get up. He could wallow in self-pity, or he could make the most of things. He took a quick inventory. He was legally married to a gorgeous man—who had made it abundantly clear he didn't want to have any sort of physical relationship with Mateus. But it was for a noble reason, however misguided. Maybe with enough time, Mateus could convince him that it wouldn't be taking advantage of anything for the two of them to give in to their obvious mutual attraction. And maybe it could lead to something more.

God. What was this, a Disney movie? Of course it wouldn't lead to anything more. The situation was already ridiculous and extraordinary on its own. And fairy tales, the real ones, usually ended up with dead mermaids and stepsisters who cut off their own toes. Not forest creatures cleaning houses and kisses from Prince Charming.

Mateus needed to take care of practicalities before he let himself freak out over the situation he was in. For one, he was out of clean clothes. There was a boutique downstairs, but it looked so high-end he probably couldn't even afford a pair of briefs there. So he'd have to venture out and find a mall or something. A Walmart or Target would be even better, but he didn't like his chances of facing off against Davis again wearing a three-dollar T-shirt. He wasn't going to be an embarrassment for Crawford, which meant he'd have to find a way to swing some decent clothes.

Crawford had made it abundantly clear that he didn't have to worry about the cost of the hotel room or food while he was there since it was Crawford's fault they were stuck in Vancouver for the next however long. That wasn't the view Mateus took of it, but he appreciated the generosity. So at least he didn't have to worry about meals, though he was determined to pay Crawford back for all this someday. Probably some *someday* far in the future, but Mateus wasn't going to let the kindness go unpaid.

Duarte had offered to send him some money when they'd spoken last night, but he and Bree couldn't afford that, and Mateus didn't want to stretch their already thin budget any further. Maybe he could have them ship some clothes to him, though. He'd brought all of his clothes with him when he'd come to the States three months ago. He still had furniture and other things in storage in Lisbon, but he'd known even then that it was unlikely he'd be returning home at the end of his three-month visa. He just hadn't imagined how many hoops he'd have to jump through to make that happen.

Convincing Duarte he hadn't been kidnapped by a psychotic Canadian who wanted to harvest his organs had been difficult. He'd told his brother that his visa had been reset as soon as he'd entered Canada and that he'd met someone interesting on the plane and decided to stay in Vancouver with him for a bit to blow off some steam. Duarte had been suspicious, but after Mateus had promised to check in at least once a day, he'd loosened up and sounded so happy Mateus was having fun that Mateus had been eaten up by guilt after he'd hung up. He hated lying to Duarte and Bree, but if he told them the truth, they'd insist on getting involved, and they definitely couldn't afford an immigration lawyer. The barn needed a new roof, and that was the priority right now. That and the baby.

Mateus jumped when he heard a doorbell ring throughout the suite. A light over the elevator flashed.

He hurried over to it and pressed the call button, then stepped back in surprise when it opened and the bellman from yesterday stepped into the room.

"I wouldn't normally bother a guest who had the Do Not Disturb engaged, but Mr. Hargrave told me it was urgent you get this message from him," the man said.

He held out a tray with a cream-colored note on it, and Mateus had to bite his lip to keep from laughing. This was like every over-the-top telenovela he'd ever watched with his avó. Did rich people actually live this way? How much did this penthouse suite *cost*, anyway? Not that Crawford was footing the bill either, but still. He had the feeling that the nightly price tag for this place was higher than his monthly rent on the apartment he was currently subletting in Lisbon.

"He asked me to wait for a response," the bellman said apologetically.

Seriously?

Mateus couldn't hold back his snicker, but he took the creamy linen note and opened it.

Mateus,

Davis has arranged for us to have dinner with the hotel's general manager and some local business bigwigs. I am so, so sorry. I understand if you choose to skip it, but I would be extremely grateful if you'd come.

CH

Mateus blinked at the spiky handwriting. There were no hesitant marks or swirls and loops—the letters were well-formed and neat, but undeniably the work of a man who had little time and less patience. Crawford didn't seem to have much time or energy for niceties. He was all action. Mateus shivered, then scolded himself for getting worked up over handwriting. He was getting carried away in the telenovela fairy tale.

The bellman was still looking at him expectantly, so Mateus stuffed the note in his pocket and tried his best to look calm and assertive. He was fairly sure he failed, but it was the thought that counted.

"Tell him I'd be happy to attend," he said, even though that couldn't have been further from the truth. But it would be good practice for their immigration interview, and it would likely piss Davis off, which was a definite plus. He just couldn't see Crawford married to someone who was so smarmy. "Do you have any details about where we're going?"

He definitely didn't have anything in his suitcase that would do for a dinner that merited a handwritten invitation delivered on a silver tray. Given the state of his clothes after traveling in them yesterday and shaking them out this morning, he probably didn't even have anything appropriate for another trip to Tim Hortons.

"I believe Mr. Franklin arranged for a table at Cioppino's. A car will pick you and Mr. Hargrave up at seven thirty."

Mateus did some quick math. It was just after four now, so he had enough time for a quick shopping trip. He rubbed a hand over the stubble he hadn't bothered with this morning. A shower and a shave wouldn't go amiss either.

"Mr. Hargrave said you probably needed clothes for tonight," the man continued. "I have a cab downstairs waiting for you. The concierge made an appointment for you with a personal shopper at Hudson's Bay."

How was he going to swing this? Hell, Mateus probably couldn't even afford the cab fare, let alone the kind of store that offered personal shoppers. But how could he decline without making it obvious he didn't have that kind of money?

"Actually, I'd prefer to go shopping on my own," Mateus said, flashing the bellman a smile. "But please thank the concierge for his trouble."

The man hid a laugh with a harsh cough. "Excuse me, sir. Of course. And the cab?"

Mateus bit his lip, weighing his options. He had absolutely no idea where he was, but the cab would significantly eat into his budget.

"If I may, could I make a suggestion?" the bellman said.

"Please."

The man met his eye and, after a moment, seemed to relax a bit. His posture was still perfect, but not quite as ramrod straight as it had been just seconds ago. "So I'm guessing you're not a designer kind of guy? No offense. I'm not either." Mateus bobbed his head in agreement. "Well, then, there's a perfectly nice mall about four blocks north of here. You can't miss it. You just go out the front door, turn left, and head up a few blocks. It has some department stores, and I'm sure you'd be able to find something there. Cioppino's is pretty fancy, but there isn't a formal dress code like there is at the restaurant here. You won't get tossed out if you show up without a blazer."

He eyed Mateus, and Mateus fought the urge to hide behind something. It was clinical, not sexual, but it still made Mateus feel like he was being stripped bare. "My sister is the manager at H&M, if that isn't too lowbrow for you. I could call her and see if she could help."

It wasn't his usual style, but the price would be right. "That would be amazing. I don't know much about clothes, and I don't want to embarrass Crawford."

The bellman smiled. "I don't think you could. I heard him talking about you and your brother's orchard when I helped room service deliver lunch to the conference room. He's pretty besotted." The man's cheeks dimpled when he cringed. "I shouldn't have shared that. It's not professional to talk about what we hear in the conference center. But I didn't want you to think that Mr. Hargrave isn't proud of you."

Mateus didn't know how to respond to that. He felt oddly protective of Crawford, so it shouldn't have been such a surprise that Crawford felt similarly toward Mateus, but it was.

"Thanks," Mateus said, his anxiety melting away with the genuine smile the man gave him. He started to grab his wallet—wasn't that what rich people did? Tip the people who helped them?—but the bellman shook his head.

"Mr. Hargrave already tipped me downstairs," he said. He tucked the silver tray under his arm.

Mateus let his arms drop to his sides awkwardly. "Ah. Well, thanks again," he said. "What's your sister's name?"

"Julie," he said. He held out his free hand for Mateus to shake. "I'm Max. Will you be leaving right away? I'll call to tell her to expect you, Mr. Fontes."

"Mateus, please," he said. "I make it a rule that anyone who talks me through a clothing crisis calls me by my first name."

Max laughed. "Julie will make sure it's not a crisis."

Mateus grabbed his key card from the table near the elevator and stepped up beside Max when he pressed the call button. "I doubt that. Have you seen Crawford? It's hard to compete with that level of perfection."

He'd been wearing a vest under his suit coat this morning. A vest. Mateus had felt faint, and it hadn't just been nerves over their meeting with immigration. Crawford had looked absolutely edible.

"He does cut a nice figure," Max said agreeably. He gave Mateus another side-eyed glance. "But you do too. You're a very handsome couple."

Mateus flushed. God, how he wished that were true. How was he going to make it through a fancy dinner playing Crawford's adoring husband when Crawford was dressed like someone straight out of Mateus's fantasies? He hadn't been able to keep his eyes off Crawford at the office this morning. Even the immigration officer had commented on how in love they seemed.

At least his crush was good for something. Anyone with eyes could see how attractive Mateus found Crawford, and he was vain enough to admit that he'd caught Crawford looking at him a fair few times as well.

"Thank you," Mateus said. The elevator dinged and the two of them stepped into the empty car. "And thanks for asking your sister to help me."

Max grinned. "She loves dressing pretty men. She'll be thanking *me*."

MATEUS straightened his collar and gave himself a critical look in the mirror. The black slacks Julie had picked out for him were more formfitting than he was used to, but he had to admit they looked good. She'd paired them with a crisp lavender shirt and a charcoal-gray waistcoat that he'd wanted to hate because it was so far outside his clothing comfort zone, but he'd actually kind of fallen in love with it.

Getting rid of his scruff had been a harder proposition. Julie had pointed him to a drugstore in the mall, so he'd been able to get a decent razor and some shaving foam along with toiletries for his unexpected vacation. It had taken him an embarrassing amount of time to get the kind of close shave he was used to having with his electric razor, but he was proud of the fact that he hadn't cut himself in the process.

He heard the elevator open, and a moment later Crawford called out.

"Mateus? Are you in here?"

Mateus stuck his head out of the bathroom. "Just about ready. Max said this place was fancy. Does this work?"

Crawford stumbled when he saw Mateus. The naked lust on his face was gratifying, but it was all the more frustrating to see it shuttered behind the polite smile Mateus was coming to hate. He didn't want to be another person Crawford had to put on a false front for.

Mateus wanted that look back. He spun around, showing off his outfit. "Will this do? I wasn't sure if it was fancy enough, but Julie said it was."

"Who's Julie? And Max?" Crawford asked gruffly. Had that been a tinge of jealousy?

Satisfaction rushed through Mateus, making him bold. "Max told me we made a handsome couple, so I had to live up to my end of that," he said. He definitely hadn't been imagining things. Crawford's jaw twitched. Mateus took pity on him. "Max is the bellman who brought me the message. Julie is his sister. She helped me pick this out," he said, motioning toward his outfit.

"The personal shopper? I didn't think you'd go for that, but Davis insisted. I guess he's worked with her before."

Mateus laughed. "God, no. I had Max cancel that. Julie works at the mall."

Crawford's eyes darkened as his gaze swept up and down Mateus's clothes. Heat bubbled up out of Mateus's stomach at the raw male appreciation that Crawford wasn't doing anything to hide at the moment. "You got that at the mall?"

Mateus's chest was full of butterflies. "Is it okay?"

Crawford's full lips finally curved up into a smile. "It's more than okay. You look gorgeous." Mateus held back the temptation to pump his fist in victory, but only just barely. That was a big admission from Crawford. Maybe things were looking up. "Davis is going to be green with envy."

Mateus's spirits sank. He hadn't thought Crawford was still hung up on his ex-husband, but maybe he was. Maybe this fake marriage would end up getting their real one back together. He wouldn't stand in the way of that, not if it made Crawford happy. "Ah. Well, then, we shouldn't keep him waiting."

Confusion flitted across Crawford's face. "The car's not due for another ten or fifteen minutes. I was going to freshen up a bit."

Mateus hoped that didn't involve taking the vest off. He watched as Crawford deftly undid his tie and tossed it on the sofa. He had to look away when he started working on the buttons at his throat. He'd probably embarrass himself if he saw much more of that deliciously tanned skin revealed. Crawford looked like a high-powered businessman who'd come home to be debauched, and that was not a mental image Mateus needed.

"I talked to the manager today and asked him to move us to a different suite tomorrow," he said, disappearing into the bedroom. "I told them I didn't want to tie up their most expensive real estate for the entire trip, so they moved us down a few floors to a smaller suite. It has a bigger kitchen, so I thought we might go grocery shopping tomorrow if I can get away a little earlier. Unless you like eating room service for every meal?"

He wandered back into the main sitting area, preoccupied with buttoning the shirt he'd thrown on. He'd kept the same pants, but the vest was gone. Shame. Though the new shirt hugged his chest beautifully, so Mateus couldn't complain much.

"No, that would be great," he said when he realized Crawford was waiting for an answer.

"I get pretty tired of it," Crawford said. Mateus took a good look at him and realized how exhausted he looked. He must have spent the entire day in meetings, probably with Davis by his side.

"So dinner tonight, what's that about?"

Crawford let out a soft growl that made Mateus's skin prickle. "Davis is showboating. He has some deal he wants to pull off, and he needs the general manager and the chamber of commerce on board with it. The dinner had been planned for a while, but since we're also celebrating our wedding," Crawford said, giving up on his new tie long enough to make air quotes with an adorably exasperated look on his face, "he's inviting all their spouses too. Which is how you got dragged into it. Sorry."

Mateus shrugged. "If you can take it, I can take it. Sounds like it won't be totally boring."

Crawford gaped at him. "Davis will be schmoozing and trying to talk business all night, and we'll be stuck with a bunch of stuck-up, self-important men and their wives, who will be cooing over us all night. What about that doesn't sound terrible?"

"I didn't say it wouldn't be terrible. I said it wouldn't be boring." Especially since he planned to make it his personal mission to goad Davis into showing everyone just how oily he really was. Though that would probably be bad for Crawford in the long run. Dammit.

"Will they ask a bunch of questions about us, do you think?"

Crawford groaned. "Tons. I swear I fielded more questions about you than I did about what I was actually brought here to do," he said. He offered Mateus a tired smile when Mateus made a distressed sound. "Not your fault. And it's worlds better than getting questions about how I'm handling working with my ex, which is what I came here expecting."

Mateus cleared his throat. "And how's that going? If I can ask."

"Of course you can ask. You're one of the few people I actually don't mind talking about it with because I know you're not just looking for office gossip," Crawford said, his eyes crinkling when he smiled. He still looked tired, but not quite as defeated. "It's going as well as I could hope for. Having you here really is helping. Davis is still off-kilter, so he doesn't quite know what to do with me. It hasn't been perfect, but it's been miles better than I'd expected."

Because Davis was leaving him alone or because Davis was jealous? Mateus wished he could read between the lines and figure out if Crawford was still interested in his ex-husband. He really hoped he wasn't. Not that Mateus had any sort of claim over Crawford.

Except he kind of did, in the one way that legally mattered. He might not have Crawford's heart—and Crawford definitely didn't have his—but he had Crawford's marital status. And right now that was more important than his silly crush on Crawford and his ridiculous jealousy over a man Crawford openly loathed most of the time. What business was it of his if Crawford and Davis ended up having some sort of torrid hate-sex affair?

The thought made Mateus swallow hard. He had to bite back a question about Crawford's feelings, because he honestly didn't know if he was asking about his feelings for Davis or his feelings for Mateus. Mateus knew he wasn't the only one who felt the attraction between them, but so far he seemed like the only one even remotely inclined to act on it.

He'd have to play the doting husband tonight, so it was probably better not to get into it. He'd have a hard time smiling and flirting if Crawford told him he was using the interactions as a way to get into Davis's bed.

This could get complicated fast. They'd come up with a bare-bones story for the meeting this morning, but they'd have to spend some time coming up with a better story if they were going to get grilled by everyone. "Have you told them anything I should know? So I don't say something different?"

"Nah. I was vague." Crawford rolled his shoulders, and Mateus's fingers ached to slide over them and work out some of the tension he could see coiled there. Maybe he'd be able to talk Crawford into a massage later. Or at the very least, taking advantage of the hot tub out on the terrace. They hadn't made it out there last night, and if they were moving to a different room tomorrow, this would be their last chance.

"Will that work tonight? If these wives really are as nosy as you think they will be?"

Crawford's hands hovered over the suit coat he'd draped over the stool at the bar, but he passed it over after another glance at Mateus's outfit. He looked gorgeous, between the immaculately tailored pants and the simple Oxford shirt and the thin navy blue sweater he'd pulled over it that looked as soft as a cloud. It was a much more casual look than the three-piece suit, but he looked just as put together, like he'd stepped out of a fancy magazine.

"Eh, I figure we'll just be a little mysterious. It should be fine. Especially if we sit far away from Davis."

Mateus had figured that was a given. "Will he make that difficult?"

"Probably. Difficult is his specialty." Crawford dug through his suit coat and came up with his key card. "Do you want to go downstairs? We can grab a drink in the bar while we wait for Davis."

Mateus wasn't sure alcohol and Crawford were a good mix for him. He didn't need any loosened inhibitions, especially in front of people Crawford worked with. But surely one drink wouldn't hurt. He could do with a little loosening. He'd been tightly wound ever since Max came by to give him the summons to dinner.

"Are we riding over with Davis, then?" Mateus called the elevator and jammed his hands into his pockets just to have something to do that wasn't giving in to his temptation to reach out and see just how soft Crawford's sweater was—and how hard his chest was underneath it.

Crawford made a disgusted sound. "Yes. We could have just taken a cab, but he wanted to book a car because it would look better."

"Is tonight's dinner something your company will pay for?"

Mateus needed to know if he'd be on the hook for his own meal tonight. He wasn't going to let Crawford pay for it himself, but he certainly wouldn't turn down a free meal if it came at the hotel's expense. Especially since it was technically a business dinner. Maybe Crawford should ask for hazard pay for any time he had to spend with Davis outside the hotel. Mateus had the feeling it wasn't going to go well.

"Davis will put it on the company card, I'm sure," Crawford said dismissively, like they expensed four-figure dinners all the time. Maybe they did. Mateus really didn't know much about what Crawford did.

"Are there any topics you want to steer conversation away from? I can help with that."

"Tons. But I don't want to put you in that position. I expect most of the wives will want gossip about my divorce and how you and I met. Stick to the truth as much as possible. We met at the airport while you were coming to visit your brother, hit it off, and things went from there. Don't talk about Davis at all. God knows I won't be," he said, his smile turning grim.

Mateus hated people who gossiped about other people's tragedies to make themselves feel better. "You shouldn't have to. It's none of their business."

Crawford grinned. Mateus wanted to taste the soft curve of his bottom lip. He clenched his teeth instead. Crawford wasn't his to kiss.

"Ah, but it's human nature. The Germans even have a name for it. Schadenfreude. Taking pleasure in someone else's misfortune." Crawford's tone was chipper, like he wasn't going to be the one at the butt of any of the schadenfreude that got tossed around at dinner. How could he be so blasé? It wasn't even about Crawford, and it made Mateus want to destroy something.

"Just because it's human nature doesn't make it right," Mateus snapped.

Crawford studied him for a moment, his smile growing. "Most things about human nature aren't right. Like confusing lust for love. Luckily we learn from our mistakes. That's human nature too. And now I know not to trust anything intangible. Love doesn't exist."

"Surely you don't mean that. Love does exist. It's everywhere. And just because he hurt you doesn't mean you weren't in love with him at one time. Or that he wasn't in love with you. People change, and it's not always for the better."

Crawford shrugged noncommittally. "Everyone has a different outlook."

Mateus let the conversation drop, but he couldn't help but turn Crawford's bitter words over and over in his head as they drove to the restaurant. Did Crawford really not believe in love, or was he just hiding a tender heart behind a facade of sneering disinterest? And if he wasn't still in love with Davis, then why was he so preoccupied with making him jealous? How did Mateus fit into that?

MATEUS slumped against his seat and watched the buildings pass by out the window. Davis had been waiting for them at the car, and he and Crawford were engaged in an animated debate involving expanding the hotel's spa. He snuck a look over at them.

They looked relaxed in each other's presence. Crawford was sitting between Mateus and Davis, and Mateus couldn't help but notice he was closer to Davis than he was to him. He tried not to read too much into it, but when Davis flung a hand out to accentuate a point and let it come to rest on Crawford's shoulder, Mateus gave up on watching them and stared out the window again.

Mateus knew Crawford was attracted to him—that was obvious. So was the chemistry between them. But Crawford had chemistry with Davis too. And a history. That was a lot to overcome. Especially since Crawford had been steadfast in his determination to keep things nonsexual between himself and Mateus out of some misguided nobility that was both a turn-on and a source of never-ending frustration.

But watching him with Davis, Mateus wondered if it was more than that. Was Crawford's hesitancy just because he thought he'd be taking advantage of Mateus, or was there more to it? He'd been so adamant that love didn't exist. Maybe too adamant. Was it possible he wasn't over Davis?

Mateus hadn't known Crawford long enough to be hurt or jealous, but he didn't have any other way to explain the empty ache in his chest.

Chapter Nine

CRAWFORD should have declined. Both the dinner they'd just suffered through and Mateus's invitation to join him in their suite's rooftop hot tub afterward. It wasn't like he could blame Mateus for how he was feeling. Mateus had just been following Crawford's instructions earlier; that was the real killer. Crawford had asked him to pretend, and God, had he.

Mateus had been amazing at the restaurant. He'd been strangely quiet and withdrawn in the car, but as soon as they'd gotten to the restaurant, he'd perked up and become the embodiment of the perfect husband.

He'd been attentive and funny, and the smoldering looks he'd sent Crawford all night had been so believable Crawford was still aching from them. No one at that dinner had any reason to think he and Mateus were anything but madly in love, which was exactly what he'd wanted. The problem was that Crawford was half-convinced too, and that way lay madness.

There were a hundred good reasons not to climb into a hot tub with Mateus, and the leading one was the fact that Crawford was ridiculously attracted to his husband. Mateus had looked like perfection tonight, and he'd handled everything Davis threw at him with grace and charm. He'd completely won over everyone at their table, aside from Crawford's ex.

Crawford and Mateus had barely kept their eyes off each other all night, which had caused more than a few giggles and titters among their tablemates and obvious, seething jealousy from Davis. Instead of making him feel vindicated, it just made Crawford tired. He didn't want to play any games with Davis. He wanted nothing to do with him at all. And using someone as kind and generous as Mateus as his foil left a bad taste in Crawford's mouth. There was nothing fake about the chemistry between them, and it made Crawford's chest ache to keep up the charade as time went on.

The fact was, he was actually getting to know Mateus, and he was so much more than a pretty face and a delectable accent. He was brilliant and so passionate about the orchard he and his brother were running in Washington—Crawford could listen to him talk about it all night. Hell, he practically had. The entire table had been captivated by Mateus's stories about camping out with heaters to save the trees during an unexpected frost and his experiments with grafting saplings to try to breed out diseases. Even though he rarely indulged in anything more serious than a one-night stand, Crawford could definitely see himself in a relationship with Mateus. It was just a shame that it could never happen, given their circumstances.

At least the sexual tension between them had excused them from after-dinner drinks. If not for Mateus, Crawford would have gritted his teeth and seen the night through, but Mateus gave him a ready-made excuse to leave early. In fact, they hadn't even had to play that card themselves—the hotel's general manager had joined them for the evening, and he had practically shoved them into a cab outside the restaurant after the meal had wrapped up. It had been worth the good-natured jeers and winks to escape.

But now he was about to do something very, very stupid, so maybe it hadn't been much of an escape after all. If he were smart, he'd go to bed. He'd tell Mateus, rightly so, that he had an early meeting and needed his rest. He'd ask for a rain check so he could tackle the mountain of paperwork that was waiting for him in messy piles on the dining table. He'd fake a water phobia.

Anything that kept him out of an enclosed space in one of the most romantic settings Crawford could imagine with the one man he couldn't make a move on.

But Crawford wasn't smart. He ran through excuses in his head as he took off his clothes, carefully hung his suit in the closet, and rifled through his suitcase to find the swim trunks he knew he'd packed. Not for this occasion, of course. He'd envisioned a vigorous swim in the lap pool, not an agonizing soak in a private hot tub with the most attractive man he'd ever met.

After he changed, he picked up his phone and texted Adam, not sure whether to hope he was awake to talk him out of this or to hope that he didn't see the message in time to chastise Crawford for even thinking about it.

Rooftop hot tub with Mateus. Bad idea?

His phone dinged almost instantly.

The worst. Have fun.

Dammit.

I can't get involved with him, he texted back.

You already are. You may as well get something out of it.

Crawford took a breath and rubbed his hand over his face. As usual, Adam had cut to the quick of it and said exactly what Crawford needed to hear. It would be wrong to take advantage of Mateus. And even if Mateus said he was interested, how could Crawford be sure he really was and wasn't just saying that because he was afraid Crawford would change his mind about helping him get a visa? No. He had to keep his distance.

Thanks, bro, he texted back. He tossed his phone on the bed and strode out into the main room to tell Mateus he couldn't join him tonight. The doors to the terrace were already open, so Crawford walked through. His breath caught in his throat when he saw Mateus.

He was silhouetted against the skyline, his arms folded together like he was cold. He'd apparently picked up a pair of swim trunks at the same place he'd gotten his clothes for tonight, because they were almost indecently tight, just like the trousers he'd had on.

Crawford's excuses died on his lips. Mateus looked so breathtakingly lonely that Crawford couldn't bring himself to disappoint him. Especially when Mateus turned around and a huge smile bloomed across his face.

"Ready? I turned it on a bit ago. It should be nice and hot for us."

Mateus's eyes sparkled in the dim lights, his expression happy but still slightly unsure. Like he was expecting Crawford to bow out at any time. Would he look that vulnerable if he didn't want more from Crawford? Wouldn't he be hoping Crawford wouldn't want to spend time with him, not hoping that he'd stick around?

"I'm glad it's clear out," Crawford said, looking up. "You can't see many stars because of the light pollution from the city, but there are a few up there."

Mateus rubbed his arms briskly and came away from the edge of the terrace to join Crawford next to the hot tub. "Cold, though."

Crawford laughed. "After spending ten years in LA, anything under eighty degrees feels cold to me. I figured you'd have built up a tougher skin living in Washington. It's always chilly there."

Mateus hefted himself up onto the edge of the tub and eased into the roiling water. "Ah," he murmured as he slid deeper into the water. "That's my one complaint about the orchard. That and the rain."

"I miss rain." Crawford was trying not to stare at Mateus. But it was hard. His skin had flushed from the heat, and somehow knowing his almost-naked body was hidden underneath the water was worse than looking at him standing there in the trunks.

"Does it not rain in Los Angeles? It's on the coast, isn't it? I thought it always rained on the coast."

Crawford couldn't work up the willpower to leave, so he climbed in. It was better than standing outside the hot tub like an idiot while Mateus was in it. His skin prickled at the sudden heat, and sweat was beading on his forehead by the time he'd sunk all the way in. The water lapped at his chest, and the sharp contrast between the hot water and the cool air made his nerve endings sing. He could see why people liked to do this in cooler climates. He'd never really seen the appeal of an outdoor hot tub in LA.

"It barely rains, and when it does all hell breaks loose because everyone drives like it's the apocalypse."

"You grew up in Michigan, isn't that what you told someone at dinner? Is the weather there much different?"

The genuine interest in Mateus's voice was almost too much to take. He was everything Crawford had convinced himself didn't exist—a gorgeous, intelligent man who actually cared about him and wanted to know more about him just for the sake of getting to know him, not to dig for information that would help weasel money or favors out of him.

"It was. I do kind of miss snow. But most of the time I'm happy with the warm weather. Though palm trees with Christmas lights have always felt so wrong to me. Christmas should be for snow and sweaters, not sunshine and shorts."

Mateus smiled. "Sunshine and shorts. I like that."

"You won't get much of it in Washington."

He shook his head ruefully, making his hair flop across his face. He brushed it back with a practiced hand, a gesture that so many men Crawford knew used as artifice, but that Mateus just did without thinking. He didn't seem to have any idea how unbelievably sexy he was. Which made him even sexier.

"No, but I like sweaters. And it's so green there. It's amazing."

His face just lit up when he talked about the orchard. Crawford wished he had something like that in his life. He'd worked so hard to get where he was, but the satisfaction he used to feel was missing. Work filled his time, but it wasn't his be-all, end-all anymore. He didn't feel passionate about it like Mateus did about his trees and his plants. Crawford wanted that. He wanted to love what he did so much that he'd risk going to jail to stay in a place where he could do it. That he'd marry a stranger just to keep it for a few months longer.

"There's a rain forest on the Olympic Peninsula. Have you been?" Crawford wanted to offer to take Mateus there just so he could be the one to introduce Mateus to something so beautiful. He wanted to be there when Mateus's jaw dropped in awe and his heart swelled with happiness to be in the middle of such a magical place.

"I haven't, but I remember reading about it in graduate school. The flora in temperate rain forests has always fascinated me."

Crawford coughed and looked away before he gave in to his impulse and promised to take Mateus there. There wouldn't be any trips to lush rain forests in their future. Once they'd convinced the immigration office that their marriage was legitimate, they'd be parting ways and likely not seeing each other again. Adam had promised him they didn't even have to be in the same state to get a divorce—once the orchard was doing well enough that Duarte could hire Mateus on and make a case for a work visa, they'd just quietly sever their ties and be done with things.

It hurt even to think about. He'd only known Mateus for two days, but Crawford was becoming increasingly sure he wanted those days to be the first of many they shared. Which was why he gave in to instinct and leaned forward, his eyes on Mateus's face as he closed in, giving Mateus plenty of time to pull back if this wasn't what he wanted.

Crawford's heart sang when Mateus leaned forward himself, closing the gap between them with a small smile. Crawford closed his eyes just before their lips touched, but not before he'd gotten a close enough look to catalog all the colors in Mateus's eyes. They looked brown, but up close there were flecks of gold that sparkled in the dim light.

The kiss was tentative, and Crawford let it stay that way. He didn't want to take control, since he still wasn't sure of his welcome. After a moment, Mateus took charge, driving the kiss deeper. Crawford shivered when Mateus's tongue probed at the seam of his closed lips, and he opened them, inviting Mateus in. He tilted his head for better access, but kept his hands at his sides. He wanted to touch Mateus right now more than anything, which was why he didn't. The rational part of his brain might have disengaged enough to make the kiss seem like a good idea, but he was still present enough to know that letting things escalate would be a very bad idea.

He pulled back when Mateus broke the kiss to take a breath. He soaked in the sight of Mateus's kiss-swollen lips and the hint of beard burn from the five-o'clock shadow Crawford hadn't bothered to shave off before dinner. They stared at each other for a long moment, the bubbling of the jets competing with the roaring of his own blood in his ears to fill the silence.

"I should get to bed," Crawford blurted. Mateus's face shuttered, going back to his mask of polite interest. "I mean, it's late. And I have a breakfast meeting with Davis. So, bed."

He'd meant to say he'd enjoyed the kiss. Or that he wanted to talk about taking things to the next level between them. But he couldn't get the words past his tongue. Guilt flooded through him. What had he been thinking? He'd forgotten why they were there. This wasn't a meaningless hookup with someone he'd met in a bar, something to scratch an itch. This was his husband—the man who was only here because he had to be.

Mateus's face had closed off as soon as Crawford pulled back and started babbling, and Crawford hated that he couldn't read him. Mateus was usually so open. Seeing him sitting there with a blank expression bordered on painful, especially since Crawford was the one responsible for putting that look on his face.

Crawford hauled himself up out of the water. Steam rose off his body, and his skin erupted in gooseflesh at the sudden change in temperature. It helped tamp down the arousal that had threaded through him after kissing Mateus, finishing off the lingering tendrils of it that had remained even after his attack of guilt. How could he have done something so stupid?

"There's no one booked after us, so there's no rush to leave the room tomorrow. We could have lunch, if you like, and maybe get checked in to the new suite after that?"

He shouldn't be having lunch with Mateus. He'd planned a brutal work schedule that didn't include taking time off in the middle of the day to eat when he could be having a working lunch with Davis and the hotel's managers, but Crawford didn't like the thought of Mateus bumming around the suite all day with nothing to do. The kindest thing for both of them would be to keep his distance and establish a friendly but reserved attitude with Mateus, but Crawford just couldn't seem to do it. He'd take one step forward—like deciding not to get into the hot tub—and then two steps back. Though giving in to temptation and kissing

Mateus had probably been more than two steps back. It would probably qualify as a leap.

"I'm going to stay out here a bit longer," Mateus said, his gaze cast down at the water.

Crawford didn't have to be able to see his face to know he'd hurt Mateus. That was worse than the unemotional mask from a moment before. He needed to bite the bullet and do something about this before it spiraled out of control. He didn't want Mateus to hate him, but he also didn't want to delve into any complicated conversations when he was in this state.

"Listen, I'm sorry," he said, his heart in his throat. "I shouldn't have kissed you like that. I didn't have the right to put you in that situation. I just got carried away in the moment."

Mateus looked up, and Crawford was surprised to see he looked angry. "The moment?"

Crawford swallowed hard. "The atmosphere. I had a nice night with you, despite the company we shared it with. And sitting out here under the stars, it just felt like the right thing to do. So I apologize. I'll do better in the future, I promise."

Crawford wasn't sure what exactly he was promising with that. Was he giving his word that he would respect Mateus's boundaries and stay away? Or was he promising that next time it wouldn't be an ill-thought-out, fumbled kiss in the dark? He didn't know. The only thing he was certain of was that he needed to make his exit now, before he said anything he couldn't fix later.

"I'll see you tomorrow for lunch. If that doesn't fit into your plans, leave a message for me at the front desk, okay?"

He didn't wait for Mateus's response. It was cowardly, but Crawford was at his limit for the night.

He'd been on edge all day thanks to Davis, and then barely able to contain the urge to pounce on Mateus all evening. He'd been pushed to his breaking point, and he'd broken.

Unfortunately, it had come at the cost of Mateus's trust and his own self-respect.

Crawford grabbed a towel from the bench on the way back in, leaving the sliding door open as he walked into the suite. He needed a shower and a good night's sleep, but he was only likely to get one of them. Especially knowing how badly he'd fucked up tonight.

Crawford darted into the bedroom, gathered up his things, and shoved them haphazardly into his suitcase. If he was quick, he could snag the sofa before Mateus came inside. It was only fair, since he'd gotten the bed last night. And since he was likely to be tossing and turning the whole time anyway, it made sense. There was no reason for both of them to suffer.

He tossed his things next to the couch and used the blankets in the closet to make a small bed for himself. He added his open suitcase to the top of the pile for good measure, making it clear that he'd staked out the space for himself. Maybe Mateus would come in while he was showering and get the hint that the bedroom was his. It would probably be in both of their best interests if they didn't talk again tonight.

The suite's only bathroom connected to both the bedroom and the sitting room, and Crawford made sure to lock both doors. He didn't want Mateus coming in to confront him while he was in the shower, which was another act of self-preservation. It was hard enough to resist Mateus when he was clothed. All bets would be off if one of them was naked.

Though Mateus *had* been practically naked out there. The swim trunks he'd been wearing hadn't left much to the imagination—and Crawford had a very active imagination. He turned the shower on full blast. The hot water pounded against his chilled skin, and he had to bite back a groan of appreciation at the sensation. He didn't want to linger too long under the spray, but he indulged in a solid minute of standing with his eyes shut, just letting the heat and the water relax him. The hot tub had been nice, but he'd been so high-strung thanks to Mateus's nearness that he'd been wound even tighter when he'd gotten out than he had been going in.

Crawford tried not to think about the way the trunks had hugged Mateus's hips and framed his ass, but it was difficult. Especially knowing he was still out there, the thin fabric clinging to him in the swirling eddies of hot water.

Crawford groaned and palmed himself. He'd resisted getting himself off since this fiasco began, but he didn't think there was much hope of getting out of the shower without taking care of his growing arousal.

Chapter Ten

DESPITE having been in the comfortable bed, Mateus hadn't slept well. Crawford had already been wrapped up in a burrito of blankets on the couch when he'd come in from the hot tub last night, though he highly doubted Crawford had actually been asleep.

He'd left him in his cocoon and shut himself in the bedroom. The sheets smelled faintly of Crawford's cologne, and that, paired with how disappointed Mateus had been when Crawford had practically fled after the kiss they'd shared, had kept him tossing and turning for hours.

He finally gave up around seven thirty, figuring Crawford had already left for his early-morning meeting. Davis had said something about seeing him at seven in the hotel restaurant, so Mateus waited until he was reasonably sure Crawford would have had time to slink out of the suite.

Mateus shucked off his boxers and wrapped the towel he'd worn in from the hot tub last night around his waist. There was a coffee pot in the small kitchenette area, and all he wanted at that moment was a hot cup of coffee and a shower.

He came up short when he opened the frosted doors and saw Crawford's adorably tousled head hanging off the edge of the couch. His blanket burrito had shifted during the night, exposing a smooth bare chest that had Mateus's sleep-slow pulse speeding up.

Should he wake him? Crawford was probably late for his morning meeting, but if he was still sleeping, he probably needed the rest. His phone was on the floor next to the sofa, its LED blinking madly. It started to vibrate while Mateus was looking at it. The screen lit up with Davis's name.

Crawford had forgotten to turn the sound back on after their dinner with the bigwigs last night.

The screen went dark and then lit up again almost instantly. Davis was probably one call away from coming up to the suite himself to rouse Crawford, and Mateus didn't like the thought of that. He didn't want anyone, least of all Crawford's asshole ex, to see him like this.

He crouched down next to Crawford, one hand holding up his precariously tied towel, and tentatively touched Crawford's shoulder. It was chilly from being exposed to the morning air, and Crawford made a soft sound and scooted closer, like he was subconsciously seeking out the heat of Mateus's palm.

"Crawford," he murmured, not wanting to startle him awake. He didn't know how Crawford woke up in the morning. Was he the kind of person who came awake instantly? Or maybe he was more like Mateus, who usually swam toward consciousness reluctantly.

Crawford nestled deeper into the blankets, and Mateus sighed. A stronger approach, then.

He ran a hand through Crawford's hair, indulging himself in the need for some sort of tactile connection. It's what he wished he'd done last night when Crawford kissed him, but Crawford had pulled away before Mateus had gotten the chance. His salt-and-pepper hair was bristly under Mateus's hand, tickling the tender skin. The scruff on Crawford's chin would probably feel even better, but that was crossing a line.

"Hey, Crawford," he said, raising his voice a notch. "Crawford, you're late."

Crawford's eyes shot open, and Mateus had to brace himself against Crawford's chest to prevent himself from tumbling backward into the coffee table. Crawford's hands burst out of his cocoon and wrapped around Mateus's free wrist, steadying him.

"Whoa," Mateus muttered, his body thrumming with adrenaline from the almost-fall. Somehow he'd managed to keep his death grip on his towel, and he flushed, his skin heating with the realization that he was a flimsy piece of terry cloth away from flashing Crawford. He flexed his fingers, making sure he had all the fabric clutched tight.

Crawford blinked blearily. "You okay?" His voice was hoarse with sleep and an octave deeper than usual, which didn't help settle the flip-flopping in Mateus's stomach.

"I'm fine," he said quickly, tugging his hand out of Crawford's grasp now that he wasn't in danger of braining himself on the table. "But you're late. It's after seven thirty, and Davis has been calling."

Crawford muttered a low expletive and tossed the blankets off, revealing that he'd been sleeping in a pair of well-worn cotton boxer briefs that hugged his morning erection. Mateus's throat went dry, his gaze fixed on the delectable sight in front of him.

Crawford didn't seem to notice at all. He was a blur of motion, darting up off the couch and throwing open the suitcase he'd left on the chair next to it. "Shit, shit. We were supposed to have breakfast to go over some numbers this morning before our morning meeting."

Right on cue, his phone lit up again. Mateus picked it up and held it out to him. Crawford snatched it out of his palm and answered it in a rush. "Davis? No, I'm just late." He paused, and Mateus wished he could hear what Davis had said, because Crawford's eyes flicked over to him and then his cheeks went ruddy before he hastily broke eye contact. "That's really none of your business," he said crisply. "I'll be down in ten."

He sandwiched the phone between his ear and his shoulder and tugged on the trousers from the suit he'd worn last night, which had been draped over a chair. Mateus jogged toward the door and grabbed the blazer Crawford had left there last night to bring back to him.

"I don't care, Davis. Just order me something. You know what I like."

He hung up before Davis could respond, but the warm happiness that had been seeping through Mateus's bones at the utter domesticity of their situation evaporated at the unintentional reminder that Davis knew Crawford much better than Mateus did. He'd seen Crawford splurge on a ridiculous junk-food pretzel, and he knew his steak order thanks to dinner last night, but he didn't know what Crawford ate on a daily basis. He wouldn't have been able to order him coffee, let alone a whole breakfast.

He really needed to get to know Crawford, and fast. And not just because the immigration officer would probably ask things like what kind of cereal Crawford preferred or whether or not he took cream in his coffee. Mateus *wanted* to know those kinds of mundane things about Crawford. And maybe if they got to know each other on that level, it would be easier for Crawford to accept that Mateus wasn't returning his affection out of obligation.

Mateus watched Crawford shrug into a clean shirt and button it with an efficiency that sent another thrill through him. Crawford's motions were practiced and quick, and the simple act made Mateus wonder what else Crawford could do with those beautiful fingers.

He held out the suit coat wordlessly, a small smile playing across his lips when Crawford let him help him into it without hesitation.

Crawford ran a hand over his jaw. "Guess I'm going sloppy today," he said ruefully.

"It looks good on you," Mateus said honestly.

The stubble was a bit out of place with the sharply tailored suit, but it worked. It looked intentional.

"Good, because I don't have time to do anything about it. Thanks for waking me." He flashed a smile at Mateus. "Do you mind if I brush my teeth really quickly? Then the bathroom is yours."

Mateus glanced down at his towel and only barely resisted the urge to cross his arms over his bare chest. He was more covered up than Crawford had been a moment ago, standing there in his boxers, but he still felt extremely exposed knowing that he had nothing on under his towel.

"Go ahead," he said, uncomfortably aware of Crawford's eyes on him. He forced himself to stand up straight and keep his shoulders back instead of hunching in on himself, and he met Crawford's eye with an appreciative look of his own. Standing there in next to nothing while Crawford was completely decked out in his business suit felt illicit in the best way, and if Crawford didn't leave soon, Mateus would make a fool of himself.

He busied himself getting the coffeemaker started. The small kitchen was equipped with one that had sufficient buttons to launch itself into space, and it provided enough of a challenge to keep Mateus's mind out of the gutter while Crawford finished getting ready.

Crawford's phone started to light up again from its spot on the coffee table, and Mateus bit back a sigh. He was tempted to answer it and tell Davis to go to hell. It annoyed him that Crawford deferred to him and let Davis treat him so poorly, but it really wasn't Mateus's place to get involved. That was something a real husband would do, not a fake one.

He looked up as Crawford yanked the bathroom door open and stalked over to his phone, glaring at it before he jabbed a finger at the screen and put it up to his ear. "I said I'd be down—"

Crawford's color had already been high from rushing around to get ready, but his cheeks went even ruddier at something Davis said.

"Davis, God," he muttered. He brought a hand up and covered his eyes. "You're impossible. No, don't do that. I'm on my way."

He disconnected the call and tucked the phone into a pocket inside his coat. "Fucker," he muttered. It was more annoyed than angry, which only made Mateus more irritated himself. Why did Crawford let Davis talk to him like that?

"I don't know if I'll be able to slip away for lunch like we'd planned," Crawford said as he gathered up the papers that were stacked on the table. The apologetic tone in his voice made it seem even more domestic. Mateus had the feeling that if they really were married, his days would be filled with apologies like that. "Why don't you order breakfast and enjoy it out on the terrace? Maybe go do some sightseeing today? I'll be back for dinner. They should send the key to the new room up whenever it's ready. Don't worry about clearing out of here, we can do that after dinner tonight."

He grabbed the satchel he'd just filled with paperwork and shot Mateus a heartbreakingly earnest smile before climbing into the elevator that was already open and waiting for him. Davis had obviously had someone send it up since only someone with a room key could access the penthouse floor. At least he hadn't come up with it.

"Have a good day!" Mateus called out just before the doors closed.

He sighed and looked down at the mug of coffee he'd just brewed. Was it pathetic that he was looking forward to moving rooms just because it would give him something productive to do? He felt ungrateful for being bored in a place that offered so many amenities, but he wasn't really a sit-around-and-watch-daytime-TV kind of guy. He'd e-mailed his boss yesterday and formally resigned, and he'd skyped with the couple who was subletting his apartment in Lisbon to make arrangements for them to take over the lease permanently. His things were already in storage, so he'd have to arrange to have them sent to Washington, but he was paid up for another three months, so it wasn't a priority.

He was bored. Painfully, horribly bored.

He'd had fun rushing around getting clothes for last night's dinner, but that was mostly because Julie had been funny and he'd enjoyed hanging out with her. He wanted to go out and explore the city, but he didn't want to do it alone. Mateus had no problem with keeping his own company when he was focused on a task, but wandering around a city looking at landmarks felt empty when he didn't have anyone to share it with.

Hadn't the clerk at check-in said the concierge could book him on city tours? Mateus perked up at the thought of joining in with a group of tourists seeing the city. He'd have someone to talk to, at least. He carried his coffee with him to the bathroom. He'd shower and pack up his stuff and then head downstairs to see what could be arranged for him today. With any luck there would be a good walking tour that wasn't too expensive. Getting some exercise seemed like a good way to burn up some of the sexual frustration that seemed to be Mateus's new normal.

THERE were two new hotel key cards and a fruit basket with a card signed by the front desk staff congratulating them on their marriage when Mateus let himself back into their room after spending the afternoon walking around the city. Most of the people on the tour had been couples, but he hadn't minded. His wedding ring had gone a long way to making things less awkward. He'd even tagged along for lunch with a group from the tour, and they'd spent the afternoon at the Vancouver Art Gallery together.

It had been a nice break from the tension of being cooped up with Crawford and the ever-present Davis cloud that followed them around.

Mateus was eating a pear on the terrace when Crawford made it back. He didn't turn when he heard Crawford walk up behind him.

"I packed your toiletries up for you. The bag is on top of your suitcase."

Crawford didn't respond, so Mateus turned around and quirked a curious eyebrow at him. He looked taken aback. Mateus reviewed what he'd said and flushed a bit. He hadn't thought anything of packing up Crawford's things in the bathroom when he'd been packing his own, but he could see how that could be construed as something intimate. "I was already doing mine," he said with a shrug.

"Thanks," Crawford said after a beat. "That was nice of you. I meant to do it this morning, but you know, the running late thing."

Like Mateus needed a reminder about how adorably flustered Crawford had been this morning.

He wanted to tell Crawford so many things—that the two of them getting involved wouldn't be Crawford taking advantage of him. That he wanted Crawford, and that he'd wanted him from the first moment he'd sat down next to him in the airport with his greasy, butter-dipped monstrosity of a snack. That marriage was a big deal to him, and that he wanted to do his best to make theirs real and not just a sham. That he needed to know if Crawford's end goal was getting back with Davis because that changed everything.

But none of that came out when he opened his mouth around Crawford. Mateus just couldn't seem to force the confrontation. He was afraid Crawford might not feel the same, even though it seemed like he did. What if Crawford really didn't want him, and it wasn't a case of Crawford's overactive conscience putting the brakes on? God knew he had some messed-up ideas of what marriage actually was, thanks to Davis.

Mateus had never actively hated someone before, but he was pretty sure that was what he felt burning in the pit of his stomach whenever he saw the way Crawford shrank into himself around his ex-husband. He was still cordial and perfectly professional, and he doubted Crawford let it affect business decisions, but he was different socially around Davis. Less. Like he wanted to take up less space and not be noticed. It wasn't something Mateus liked to see on anyone, but least of all someone who was usually larger-than-life like Crawford. Davis just seemed to suck all the air out of the room where Crawford was concerned, and Mateus felt driven to do whatever he could to get him breathing again.

A lot of the questions he had weren't something he could easily sort out, but one was. Mateus bit the bullet and went in for the kill. He really couldn't take not knowing any longer. "Are you still in love with Davis?"

Crawford gave him a sharp look. "No. Why?"

His answer had been knee-jerk, and Mateus didn't know what to make of that. Was that because he was used to denying it or because he really wasn't?

"Because you were happy about making him jealous, and even though you complain about it, I can tell he doesn't annoy you as much as you pretend he does."

Crawford snorted. "Oh, trust me, he annoys me a lot more than I let on. That's how Davis works, though. He gets off on knowing that he can control people like that, so I don't let him see how much he gets to me. But he does. I gave serious thought to declining the assignment, even though it would probably have meant getting fired."

Crawford took a breath and rubbed a hand over his face. "Listen, I'm not in love with Davis. I'm not sure I ever really loved him, but I sure as hell don't now. Our divorce—it was messy. Ugly. I was in a bad place for the first year after we split. But then I realized that I was still letting him have control over me. Because of *love*." Crawford's lip curled. "I've done a lot better since realizing that love is just a way manipulative people twist lust to get what they want."

Mateus gaped at him. "That is not love. My God, Crawford, how can you be so bitter?"

Crawford leveled a flat look at him. "Davis married me to get ahead in the company and then cheated on me in my own bed pretty much every time I went on a business trip."

Mateus's heart hurt for him, but he still couldn't wrap his mind around Crawford really meaning what he was saying about love. "That doesn't mean you didn't love him. It means he's a terrible person, but it doesn't reflect on you."

"Then I'm a goddamn idiot, aren't I?"

"No. Never. But it's time to let Davis go and start putting yourself first."

Mateus wanted to hug him, but he was sure the contact wouldn't be appreciated right now. The chasm between them at the moment was much bigger than the one he'd imagined when he thought Crawford was still pining after Davis. “Love isn’t logical. It just is.” He held a hand out tentatively, and when Crawford didn’t flinch away he let it rest lightly over Crawford’s breast pocket. “We don’t fall in love with our brains. We fall in love with our hearts. You can’t shut yourself off because you were hurt.”

Crawford stalked toward the bedroom, but he left the door open as he started packing. “It’s working so far,” he called over his shoulder.

Chapter Eleven

CRAWFORD had looked over the numbers until his eyes crossed, but he still didn't see a way to make the hotel's fine-dining restaurant profitable. There were too many other similar restaurants nearby, and the hotel didn't have a celebrity chef to boost its profile. Hiring a new executive chef might work, but it would be a gamble. And since they were already taking a gamble on expanding the spa, they didn't have the leeway to make it work.

It was frustrating, because this was the last piece of the puzzle. He and Mateus had been here for more than a week, and Crawford had actually made good progress powering through his audits and meetings. No one other than Davis had complained about the accelerated schedule, and even though Crawford was exhausted from his late nights and early mornings, it would be worth it if it meant finishing up here early. Which he'd be doing, but only if he could come up with a way to make the hotel's restaurant profitable.

"I give up," he conceded, shoving his laptop away in disgust. "Fine dining isn't going to work in this location. So what do we do? Convert it to casual dining? Use the space for a coffee shop and dessert bar?"

Those were things that had worked at other failing locations, but there wasn't a lot of foot traffic out front, which meant they wouldn't draw in tourists looking for a pick-me-up. He stretched and looked over the pile of paperwork to catch Davis's eye. He looked every bit as exhausted as Crawford felt. Though he was probably sleeping better at night.

Crawford had spent last night on the pullout sofa in the sitting room of the suite he was sharing with Mateus. He'd given Mateus the bedroom when they'd moved into the new suite, since Mateus wasn't the one who needed to be up at the crack of dawn for breakfast meetings and interviews. It just made sense for Crawford to be the unlucky one who had to sleep on the lumpy sofa bed, since he'd be up early enough to clean it up and stow all the linens before the maids came to clean the room.

Mateus, he'd learned, was not a morning person. He was fairly useless before he'd had his first cup of coffee in the a.m., and even then he was mostly incoherent until he'd been up and around for a bit.

"What were the room service numbers for the last year?" Davis asked as he sifted through a pile of paperwork.

Crawford squinted at the report in front of him, his finger tracing down the column. "Not stellar. It looks like only about thirty percent of guests are ordering breakfast, and those are full meals. Maybe a coffee shop that offers light breakfast fare?"

Mateus had complained this morning about the lack of simple breakfast options on the menu. The menu was mostly full breakfasts, and the muffins and yogurts were expensive to buy à la carte.

Davis hummed thoughtfully. "There's that local chain coffee shop. Happy Bean? Java something? Some pun. Maybe they'd want to open a location here. I don't know that we could take the overhead for a coffee shop, but maybe we could rent the space out? It's an interesting idea."

"Don't sound so surprised," Crawford said dryly.

"I'm not surprised you had a good idea, I'm just surprised that you aren't arguing to keep the fine-dining space. You always argue for those."

"When it makes sense. It doesn't make sense here." Crawford didn't know why he felt so defensive. If it had been anyone other than Davis, he wouldn't have felt so attacked, but being around Davis was still too raw for him not to take everything personally.

Davis held his hands up and made a placating gesture. "I'm agreeing with you. Jesus. I hope your new boy toy doesn't mind the nagging."

Crawford took a deep breath and bit his lip. It was sore and chapped already from constantly worrying at it over the last few days, and the twinge of pain helped him keep his temper.

"Though I suppose you make up for it in other ways."

Crawford jumped when Davis's hand crept up his thigh. He stood up abruptly, knocking over the chair he'd been sitting in. They were in Davis's suite because it had a large table to work on and was more private than the conference center's boardroom, but he was regretting that decision now.

"What the fuck, Davis?"

Davis shrugged, his expression bland. "I just thought you might be up for a little fun. After all, that was never our problem. We were always at our most compatible in bed."

Crawford's lips curled in disgust. "You're compatible with everyone in bed," he snapped. "And I'm married, asshole."

Davis's Cheshire grin made Crawford's stomach turn. "That's never been an issue for me."

"I remember," Crawford growled. He slammed his laptop shut with more force than was probably advisable and hooked his hand around the strap of his satchel, not bothering to gather up the papers he swept off the table with it. "I'm going to work in my suite. I'll feel out Sacred Grounds to see if they're interested."

Davis snapped his fingers. "I *knew* it was a pun!"

Crawford shook his head, still seething. This was exactly why he hadn't wanted to work with Davis. He had absolutely no moral compass, and he was a complete jackass too. "If you need something from me, email. We have a meeting with the management staff tomorrow morning. I don't want to see you before then."

He turned when he reached the door, his muscles so tense they quivered. "If you ever touch me again, I'll break your hand," he said, holding eye contact with Davis so Davis could see he was serious. "And I don't want you near Mateus. Leave him alone."

Davis rolled his eyes. "Worried he might stray so soon?"

Crawford gritted his teeth and left, resisting the urge to slam the door behind himself, but only just barely. He bypassed the elevators and took the stairs the four floors up to his own suite, but he was still shaking with anger by the time he let himself in. Mateus was lying on the sofa with a book, and Crawford brushed off his startled hello with a growl.

He'd dug his running clothes out of his suitcase by the time Mateus appeared in the bedroom doorway. He still had the stupid book in his hand, and he looked wide-eyed and confused. Crawford wanted to jump him and kiss the concerned look off his face, which was exactly why he was going running.

He hadn't evaluated the hotel's fitness center yet, so he'd justify disappearing midday as a facilities inspection. He usually liked to work out in the hotel gym to see how well the setup worked and how well-used it was among guests, so it wasn't like he was actually slacking off. But if he'd stayed in that room with Davis another minute he'd have broken something, and he was in no place to do anything that required any sort of concentration.

Mateus didn't shift aside when Crawford moved toward the door. He stood his ground, meeting Crawford's eye with an almost defiant glare. "What happened?"

"Nothing happened, I just want to go for a run." Crawford closed his eyes and took a breath to calm himself before he said something he'd regret. Mateus wasn't the one he was mad at, after all. It wasn't fair to take out his anger on him. Especially since he was obviously just trying to help. "Davis," he said flatly. "Davis happened."

Mateus sucked in a breath through his teeth. "Are you all right?"

Some of the tension went out of Crawford's body at the way Mateus was sizing him up, obviously looking for any sort of injury. "Just my pride," he said, deflating further when Mateus looped an arm around his shoulders and pulled him in for a hug.

"I'm sorry," Mateus said quietly. His breath puffed against the shell of Crawford's ear, making the tiny hairs on his neck stand at attention. It felt so good to be held like this again. Intimacy wasn't something he'd experienced much of since Davis. Casual hookups were good to scratch most itches, but they didn't provide much comfort.

"Not your fault." Crawford let himself relax into Mateus's embrace when it became clear that Mateus didn't intend for the hug to be quick.

"What did he do?"

Crawford felt ashamed to admit that an unwanted touch from his ex could make him so upset, but he didn't want to lie to Mateus. "Felt me up."

Mateus stiffened. "That—"

Crawford shushed him. "It's fine. He didn't get far, and I let him know in no uncertain terms that if he ever touched me again, he'd be sorry."

"He shouldn't have touched you in the first place." Mateus gave him a squeeze and let him go. Crawford almost stumbled at the loss. He felt less like he was about to fly apart at the seams, but still angry and hurt. And now confused on top of everything. Why did Mateus feel so safe? Crawford rarely let his guard down around anyone, but Mateus worked his way past his defenses every time, effortlessly.

"You're right. But Davis is an ass, so I should have expected it. And he didn't do any actual harm. Just pissed me off."

Mateus gave him a stern look. "He did do harm. He touched you without your consent. He made you feel threatened. You should file sexual harassment charges against him. Surely your company doesn't support that kind of behavior?"

Revulsion roiled in Crawford's stomach at the thought of George or anyone else knowing that Davis had come on to him. "No," he said, shaking his head. "I'll handle it myself."

"If he did it to you, he probably does it to other people."

Davis was smarter than that. He knew he'd rile Crawford up with the touch—either to goad him into bed with him or just piss him off. Davis was an opportunist. He wouldn't have tried something like that with anyone else.

"I doubt it. But I'll watch him," Crawford said, yielding under Mateus's disapproving look. "If he steps one foot out of line with any of the other staff, I'll report him in a heartbeat."

Mateus frowned but didn't push. He seemed scarily good at knowing where Crawford's boundaries were. He stepped back, his book still in his hand.

"I'll be here when you get back from your run if you want to talk."

Crawford really, really didn't. But he was touched that Mateus was so concerned about him.

"Thanks." He balled his running shorts and T-shirt up and waved them at Mateus as he made his way to the bathroom to change. "But pounding out a few miles on the treadmill will do wonders. I'll need to work some more today, but maybe we could go out and grab some dinner later?"

Mateus watched him solemnly for a moment before he nodded. "Sure."

Crawford offered him what he hoped was a reassuring smile. “We’ll stop for coffee on the way back. I need to check out Sacred Grounds. I’m thinking about seeing if we can house a franchise here. You can try their cinnamon latte and let me know what you think.”

Mateus grinned. “And you’ll have something with more sugar than coffee.”

Crawford shrugged. “For research’s sake,” he said as he shut the bathroom door.

Mateus’s laugh rang through the wood, bringing a real smile to Crawford’s face. He caught sight of himself in the mirror, and he couldn’t remember the last time he’d felt so light and happy. He dropped his clothes on the counter and blew out a breath. Bantering with Mateus was entirely too easy. It felt comfortable and natural, just like knowing how Mateus took his coffee and that later, when Crawford suggested restaurants, Mateus would pick a place that was close enough to walk to because he liked being outside.

As they got to know each other, Crawford couldn’t help but want to go deeper and learn more about Mateus. It was well beyond friendly interest. There was no denying he was attracted to Mateus, but it was starting to feel like more.

He definitely needed that run.

Chapter Twelve

"I DON'T know what lit a fire under your ass, but I can't complain. You're slated to be in Vancouver for another week, but I agree with the report you sent. There's no reason for you to stay. The management team there can implement the plan, and Davis said he's happy to stay to oversee the contract with Sacred Grounds, so you're clear to head home. Do you need Helena to change your flight?"

Crawford doubted that George didn't know exactly why he'd worked so hard to finish up early, given the hissy fit he'd thrown in George's office a few weeks ago about being forced to work with Davis. But he let it pass without comment. "No, I already arranged it." It would have been hard to explain the necessity for a long layover in Seattle to George's assistant.

"Well, I guess I'll see you—"

"I don't have anything else on my calendar for the next week, so I figured it would be a good time to take some of that time off I've accrued, actually."

George made a noncommittal noise. "There's the—"

"I'm taking the week," Crawford said firmly. He had almost two months of vacation time stored up, and he intended to start using it. First, with this week so he could get Mateus back to his brother's orchard, and then, to go visit Adam in Japan after he got settled in, maybe in a month or two. It was time to stop using work as a crutch and actually start doing things he liked to do again.

He didn't know if it was spending time in close proximity to Davis or if it was the gentle lectures Mateus had subjected him to over and over, but Crawford was starting to realize that he'd been letting himself drift through his life since the divorce. Probably even before that. He was more than his career—especially since he didn't even like what he was doing now that he'd been promoted up into top-level management. It was too far removed from what had drawn him into the business in the first place.

"All right." George sounded taken aback. Probably because he was used to Crawford being such a yes-man. That was going to change. He was going to cut back on the travel and delegate more to his staff to free up his time for the kinds of projects he wanted to work on. Not that he knew what those were, but he'd figure it out. Mateus had told him it was time for Crawford to start putting himself first, and he was embracing that.

He looked over at the sofa, where Mateus was cramming all his new clothes into his carry-on bag. Maybe Crawford should go down to the store in the lobby and buy him a duffel. Most of the things they sold at the hotel were tasteful, but there was a luridly colored bag with the word Vancouver written on it over and over again in a rainbow of colors that was both ridiculous and absolutely perfect for Mateus.

Crawford shifted the phone, sandwiching it between his cheek and his shoulder as he folded a suit coat and layered it into his suitcase. It would have to be dry-cleaned when he got home, so he wasn't as worried about wrinkles as he had been on the way here. "I'll be available by e-mail if you really need me, but I won't be in the office until next Monday. Davis has my number. He'll call if anything comes up here, but I'm not expecting any trouble."

Davis was under strict instructions not to call unless there was a real emergency, and even then Crawford had strongly encouraged Davis to have one of the hotel staff call to relay the message instead of calling himself. Crawford didn't think anyone would object. He and Davis hadn't been alone together since the incident in Davis's room last week, and the tension had been evident to everyone on staff. Crawford had been nothing but icily polite, and Davis, true to form, had needled him every chance he got. But he hadn't touched him again, and he'd steered clear of Mateus whenever their paths crossed in the lobby, and that was about as much as Crawford could hope for.

"This spontaneous vacation doesn't have anything to do with your new husband, does it?"

Crawford squeezed his eyes shut and prayed for patience. He'd expected word to get back to George, but after the first week had passed without any comment from him, Crawford had foolishly hoped he'd been wrong. Apparently not.

"Yes, Mateus and I will be taking some time to be together," he said as cordially as he could. Mateus looked up at the mention of his name but went back to his task when Crawford rolled his eyes and shook his head.

"So congratulations are in order, then? I wasn't sure what to make of it when Davis relayed the news. It seems a bit sudden."

Of course it had been Davis. "Not really," he said, forcing himself not to snap. It wasn't really any of George's business. Why would it be? They weren't friends. George had never expressed any interest in Crawford's personal life before, aside from a few pointed inquiries about his well-being after the divorce when he and Davis had a few heated scenes on conference calls before their coworkers learned to meet with them separately.

"I didn't realize you were seeing anyone. I'm happy for you." He sounded about as thrilled as someone talking about a dentist's appointment, but Crawford wasn't offended. He just wanted to get him off the phone so he and Mateus could finish packing and get on the road before dark.

"I appreciate that. I'll see you next week."

He hung up before George could draw the conversation out any longer. It was probably bad form, but he didn't care. George hadn't shown him any consideration when he'd sent him on this assignment, so Crawford didn't really feel like he owed George any now.

He tossed his phone on the bed and watched as Mateus sat on his bag to try to zip it.

"I could get you a duffel," he offered. Mateus was slightly sweaty and flushed from his struggle with his luggage, and he looked absolutely edible. Running down to the gift shop would be a good excuse to put some distance between them before Crawford did something he'd regret.

Mateus huffed. "I'll make it fit."

The imagery those words conjured made Crawford choke.

"Throat's dry," he rasped when Mateus came over to investigate. Mateus gave him a few hard thwacks against his back and disappeared into the bathroom. He returned a few seconds later with a glass of tap water.

It was warm, but the drink he took was still soothing. At least until Mateus finished the glass when Crawford handed it back to him. It was so absentmindedly intimate—like they'd been together for years. Like they were married for real.

He never shared drinks with Davis. Davis had been big on cleanliness and not sharing germs, which was ironic considering how indiscriminate he was about where he stuck his dick. Crawford had never realized what a turn-on it would be to casually share a drink.

Or maybe it was just that anything Mateus did was a turn-on.

"Feeling better? You still look a little…." Mateus trailed off and made a vague gesture with his hand.

Crawford coughed again and rubbed a hand across his chest. "No, I'm fine. You about ready?"

Mateus nodded. "I have everything. Did you have any work you needed to finish up before we leave?" He gave Crawford a searching look. "We could stay, you know. If you still have things to do here. I appreciate you cutting your trip short to take me back, but I'll be okay here for a few more days if you need to stay."

And there he went being stupidly selfless and kind again. Crawford rubbed at his chest. It would be best to get Mateus home so he could get away from him. Not that he didn't love his company—he did. Too much. Some space would be good.

"I have time off coming, so it's no problem. And you're doing me a favor by giving me a good reason to cut the trip short. The less time I have to spend with Davis, the better."

Mateus's face twisted into an adorable scowl at the mention of Davis's name. "I'll be happier with you away from him too."

Crawford was a grown man. He had an investment portfolio. Hell, he had an accountant he actually enjoyed talking to. He should not turn to mush because Mateus was being so protective.

He busied himself with doing a sweep of the bedroom and bathroom to make sure he'd grabbed everything. Crawford wasn't used to feeling so *fond*, and it was killing him. He had Adam, Brandon, and Karen. He had friends—okay, business acquaintances—he played basketball with on the weekends and went camping with once or twice a year. He was fine. He didn't need Mateus.

Which was fortunate, because he didn't *have* Mateus. They were tied together on paper only. And the sooner Crawford got Mateus back to his own life, the better chance Crawford had of remembering that instead of becoming some pining, ridiculous fool.

Crawford looked at his watch. He had a regular Skype date with his nephew whenever he was on the road on a Monday, but Brandon wouldn't be looking for him until tonight. With any luck he'd be back in Los Angeles in time to stop by and take him to dinner instead. He and Karen were flying out for Japan soon, and Crawford didn't want to miss out on any opportunities to be with him before he left. Maybe he could use his week off to help Adam pack up things to ship.

HE and Mateus were technically supposed to be in different lines, but Crawford figured they should stick together to get Mateus through. He had plenty of time before his flight left Seattle for Los Angeles, so if he got tossed out of line and told to go to the US citizen line after Mateus passed through, it was fine.

They shuffled forward every time the line moved, and Crawford's nerves grew with every step. When it was Mateus's turn, Crawford dutifully stood behind the line on the floor while Mateus stepped forward and held his passport out to the guard with their marriage certificate tucked inside it. The man flicked it open, scanned it, and looked up, a frown on his face.

"Mr. Fontes, is Mr. Hargrave with you?"

Mateus gestured toward Crawford, and Crawford took that as a sign to approach the window.

"Crawford Hargrave?" the man asked, his face expressionless.

Crawford felt like he was a teenager in the principal's office. "Yes, sir."

"You and Mr. Fontes were married in Vancouver?"

"We were, a little over a week ago," Mateus chimed in. He still had a smile on his face, but it looked strained.

The guard hummed and pulled Mateus's passport fully into his cubicle.

"Please step out of line," he said. He pointed toward an area with a metal detector and a few bored-looking guards.

Crawford looked over at Mateus and tried to tamp down the panic building in his stomach. This was insane. How had he thought they'd get away with this?

God, Adam was going to be insufferable over this. The only experience Crawford had with jail was watching police procedurals on television, but he was reasonably sure he was allowed one phone call.

"Sir?" The agent looked at him expectantly, and Crawford realized he'd been standing there in paralyzed silence. "Please step over to the officers behind the yellow line."

Crawford swallowed past his dry throat and nodded. "Of course."

The guard slid the window on his booth shut and walked out, still holding Mateus's passport in his hand. "Ladies and gentlemen, this window is closed."

The crowd behind them murmured and balked, but the guard didn't pay them any attention. He dragged a sign out from behind the booth with an arrow directing the line to move to the booth to the left.

Mateus reached over and put a hand on Crawford's wrist, squeezing slightly. "We'll be fine."

Crawford bit down hard on his lip and followed the guard toward the space behind the yellow line. The guards had perked up and were watching the three of them approach with unconcealed interest, which couldn't be good. He didn't want to be their entertainment for the day. That sounded like it would take a lot of time and be unpleasant.

The pressure in his chest built with every foot they advanced forward. Now that they were closer, he could see two of the guards had muzzled dogs on leashes at their sides. There was a small office with a glass front behind them. The door label said Interrogation. Crawford tried not to hyperventilate.

They reached the area a few steps behind the guard, who had already ducked his head to confer with two others, Mateus's passport open in front of them. It felt anticlimactic. No one ran up to them with a gun drawn, at least.

"I think we're supposed to go back there to the office," Mateus said. His hand was still resting against Crawford's wrist, warm and comforting even through his shirt cuff.

"What if we're supposed to stay here and we end up getting shot because we moved beyond the yellow line?"

Mateus sighed. "I don't think anyone's getting shot. The worst they'd do is issue you a citation." He cast a sidelong glance at Crawford. "Though if you act this twitchy they're going to think you've got something to hide. Do you *want* a cavity search?"

Crawford let out a startled laugh. "Well, that would be one way to get some action."

Mateus grinned. "I have offered you action, you've just declined."

"Chivalrously declined," Crawford said. Mateus's teasing had helped him get a handle on things, just like he was sure Mateus had intended. He wasn't usually this brash.

"Indeed," Mateus said, inclining his head. "So shall we go in so they can start the cavity searches?"

Crawford's lip throbbed, which helped him stay centered. He made himself take a deep breath. "You're getting one now too?"

"It hardly seems fair for you to be the only one getting any action. This *is* our honeymoon, after all."

The sad part was that their honeymoon had been awesome. He'd gone to Jamaica with Davis for theirs, and they'd spent a week sunburned, drunk, and naked. And it still hadn't been as much fun as his platonic version with Mateus.

God, he was pathetic.

"Fair enough." Crawford let Mateus guide him toward the knot of guards. Even though no one seemed to be watching, he tried to keep his movements nonthreatening and obvious.

"We aren't walking toward sudden death. You don't have to look so serious." Mateus poked him in the ribs as they made their way to the glass-encased office, making Crawford flinch and then panic that the sudden movement would be viewed as a threat.

"We might be walking toward your sudden deportation. How can you not be serious?"

Mateus slid his hand down Crawford's wrist and grabbed his hand, pulling him to a stop. "Whatever happens, happens. Me? I think we'll be fine. And if we're not, we'll deal with that. I appreciate everything you've done for me, Crawford. I promise I won't let you go to jail for it."

Crawford noticed that Mateus didn't say anything about keeping himself out of jail, just Crawford. Maybe he was taking this seriously. It was hard to tell with his perpetual smile and easygoing attitude. The Suzy Sunshine act would be grating on just about anyone else, but it wasn't an act for Mateus. It was one of the things Crawford loved about him.

Shit. Loved? He hardly knew him. He didn't love him. Love didn't exist. He wasn't going to let himself confuse lust with love again, especially for someone like Mateus, who was dependent on him.

"Let's not mention the J-word in there," Crawford said with a nod over his shoulder.

"Deal. I hope the customs agents agree," Mateus joked. He took Crawford's hand and tugged him toward the door. "Showtime."

The guard from the booth turned as they approached and waved them toward the door, just as Mateus had predicted. "Someone will be in to talk with you in a few minutes. Make yourselves comfortable in the waiting room."

Mateus grinned at Crawford. "Does that sound like something someone who was about to give you a body-cavity search would say? See? We're fine."

Crawford scoffed as Mateus held the door open for him. The waiting room was empty, and there was a television playing Fox News in the corner. At least it was on mute. That was the first thing to go Crawford's way since they'd gotten off the plane.

"We are not fine," Crawford muttered. "We are in an office marked Interrogation, for God's sake."

"At least it's not a holding cell!"

Crawford couldn't help but laugh at Mateus's chipper tone. "I'll give you that."

He started to bite his lip again, but Mateus reached over and cupped his chin. "Stop that. You're about to make it bleed. They probably just want to ask us a few questions." His brow furrowed. "You won't miss your flight, will you?"

Crawford reflexively worried at his lip as soon as Mateus released him, but he stopped when Mateus made a displeased clucking sound. "I'm nervous," Crawford muttered with a petulant jut of his swollen lower lip.

"I know, but I happen to like your lip in one piece, so please don't." Mateus eyed Crawford's lips, his eyes darkening. "It's a nice lip."

Crawford let out a startled laugh. Mateus was flirting with him *now*? Was it just to get Crawford's mind off the impending train wreck, or did he actually mean it?

Before he could question him on it, the door swung open and a different guard from the one they'd talked to before walked in. He had Mateus's passport in one hand and their marriage certificate in another.

"Mr. Hargrave? Mr. Fontes? If you'd come with me, please."

They followed him down a short hallway to a closed door, which he rapped his knuckles against once. It opened a few seconds later, and the woman behind it had a different badge on her breast pocket. Immigration Services. They'd gotten to the big guns.

"Come in, gentlemen," she said, sweeping the door wider so they could step inside. The office was clearly shared by several people. It was devoid of any type of personal decoration aside from the nameplate on the desk that identified the woman as Officer Denise Charon.

Officer Charon took the seat behind the desk, and Crawford and Mateus gingerly made their way into the plastic chairs in front of it. "Do you know why we pulled you aside today?"

She had their marriage certificate in her hand. It seemed so insubstantial, but it was the only thing keeping Mateus in the country. And the two of them out of jail, depending on how much of a stickler for the rules whoever they were dealing with was.

Crawford eyed Officer Charon. Her slacks had been so sharply pleated they had to be starched—who did that anymore? She looked like a rule stickler.

"Uh, I'm not exactly sure." His voice sounded steady, which was good.

Officer Charon looked at the two of them dubiously. "What is the nature of your relationship with Mr. Fontes?"

"We—"

"We're married," Mateus said hotly, cutting him off. He leveled a pointed glare at the marriage certificate. "Obviously."

Crawford didn't think getting defensive was going to help them. He reached out and closed his hand over top of Mateus's, lowering his hand, which he'd been gesturing with. He pulled it closer and bent his head, softly kissing his knuckles. Out of the corner of his eye, he saw Mateus deflate, turning his gaze from the desk to Crawford, his face softening.

Crawford could guess what the immigration officer was asking. She clearly wanted some sort of physical demonstration that they were a couple. He scooted closer to Mateus, letting their legs bump together. He had to give Mateus credit—he was excellent at picking up cues. He twined his arm through Crawford's, bringing them even closer together.

The desk phone rang, and Officer Charon muttered an apology before picking it up. She took her eyes off them, riffling through a folder on the desk and answering questions for the person on the line.

He understood why what he and Mateus were doing was necessary, but the idea of putting on some sort of peep show in an interrogation room made Crawford's neck prickle with sweat. Luckily, Mateus seemed to know exactly what he was thinking, because he tugged Crawford closer and went in for a kiss before Crawford could chicken out.

Crawford had expected a peck on the lips, like the cursory kisses they'd exchanged for Davis's benefit at the hotel. Just something to show that they were comfortable inside each other's personal space, something quick and intimate that implied a familiarity with each other's bodies they didn't actually have. A married person's kiss. The kind of kiss couples exchange when they know they can kiss each other whenever they like, so there's no reason to be anything more than perfunctory.

That was not the kind of kiss he got. Mateus's lips were soft, and they dragged against Crawford's swollen and sore bottom lip, tentative at first and then bolder once Crawford returned the gesture. Mateus tilted his head and brought a hand up to curl into the short, bristly hair at the nape of Crawford's neck, his warm fingertips chasing away the chill of anxiety.

Crawford had indulged in a few fantasies about what having Mateus wrapped around him would feel like, but he hadn't done him justice in them. Their kiss in the hot tub had been amazing, but this was indescribable. Mateus was like a live wire. Crawford's lips tingled, and a thrill ran down his spine, arousal curling into his core. He'd never been this turned on by just a kiss.

Mateus's hand slid down Crawford's back, his palm blazing a trail of heat Crawford could feel through his thin shirt. Crawford wanted to arch back into the touch, but the sound of a throat clearing jarred him out of the moment.

Mateus flinched and pulled away at the same time that Crawford scooted his chair back. The officer had finished her phone call and was staring at them with an amused and indulgent smirk.

It was possible that Crawford was still a bit giddy from the kiss, because he turned and buried his face against Mateus's shoulder and started to laugh. Mateus joined in a second later, the two of them folded over each other, supporting each other as they giggled like kids.

"I'm sorry," Crawford managed when he'd gotten himself together. Mateus's arm was still twined around his torso, holding him close, and Crawford's heart caught in his throat at how easy and domestic it felt.

Officer Charon cleared her throat again. "I think that will suffice to explain your relationship," she said with a small grin. "Your passport was flagged by Homeland Security for further interviews when you reentered the country, Mr. Fontes. That's why we pulled you and Mr. Hargrave aside."

Well, that was ominous.

"We have a standard interview that newly married couples go through when visas are involved. Usually we can do that at the checkpoint, but since your file was flagged, you'll have to work with an immigration caseworker. She'll do the initial interview and also monitor you for the first year of your marriage."

That didn't sound too bad. Invasive, but not impossible. Crawford's schedule could be fairly flexible with enough notice, and God knew he had enough time off banked. As long as they had enough warning he could come to Seattle to meet with a caseworker whenever it was necessary.

"And of course, the home visit."

He shot a panicked look at Mateus. They had plenty of time before that, didn't they? "Home visit?" he repeated dumbly.

"It's a technicality. You'd be amazed at how many people think they can game the system and marry under false pretenses," she said, shaking her head. "It won't be hard for the two of you, I'm sure. We'll get it scheduled right away."

Obviously their kiss had been pretty convincing. Hell, Crawford had even convinced himself, so he knew it had been good.

The immigration lawyer they'd met with in Vancouver had made it all sound like a walk in the park. He'd started filing the mountain of paperwork Mateus would need, which Crawford was immensely grateful for. It was thanks to that quick thinking that they were even able to get Mateus across the border now. It could take weeks to get it approved, but no one along the way had expected that to be a problem.

Officer Charon slid a business card across the desk. "This will be your caseworker. You'll need to meet with her tomorrow. But don't worry. Like I said, it's to root out the people who don't really live together."

Crawford flipped the card over and read the name—Officer Kathleen Suarez. He couldn't get a feel from the name. Would she be nice like Officer Charon? Or would she be some matronly hardass who asked him what Mateus's favorite brand of toothpaste was?

Actually, he did know that. They'd had a ten-minute debate over breakfast last week about Crest versus Colgate. But still, how were they going to pass a home inspection when they didn't even live in the same state?

He felt Mateus's arm tighten around him. "Do we need to call to set up an appointment? We're headed to Beverly, and that's a bit of a drive from here."

"Her office opens at nine, and she sets aside the first part of the day to meet with couples who arrived after closing the day before. She'll be able to see you without an appointment, but I'd recommend getting there right as the office opens. If you're staying in Beverly, you might want to get a room here in Seattle for the night. Anyway, I apologize for the inconvenience. I'm sure Officer Suarez will do a great job with your case," she said brightly.

Crawford certainly hoped not.

Chapter Thirteen

MATEUS flopped down on the queen-size bed, wrinkling his nose when he bounced instead of sinking into it. This was nothing like the feather-soft beds at Chatham-Thompson Lion's Gate, though the rock-hard mattress and slick nylon coverlets were hardly a surprise for a place that rented for fifty-nine dollars a night.

Crawford had tried to book them into a nicer hotel down the street, but Mateus's pride wouldn't allow it. He'd been mooching off Crawford for too long—it was Mateus's turn to foot some of the bill for this, especially since they were stuck here overnight because of him. Unfortunately, he couldn't afford down comforters and 500-thread-count sheets. But the room did come with a free continental breakfast in the morning, which was kind of exciting.

He closed his eyes and listened to Crawford fumbling with the tiny coffeemaker on the bathroom sink. It was late, but he didn't say anything. He'd learned not to come between Crawford and caffeine, no matter what time of day Crawford was having it.

Something clattered into the sink with an echoing thud and Crawford cursed softly. Mateus peeked open one eye in time to see him angrily shoving the piece back into the coffeemaker.

"I saw a Starbucks a mile or so back. I think I'm going to give up on this and make a coffee run. You want a decaf cinnamon latte?"

So maybe Mateus hadn't been the only one taking notes on beverage preferences. He tried hard to ignore the fluttery feeling he got knowing Crawford had been paying attention that night they'd stopped at Sacred Grounds after dinner so Crawford could scope it out. Mateus knew how focused he was on his work, but not only had Crawford noticed how much Mateus had liked the cinnamon latte, he'd remembered Mateus telling him he liked sweeter drinks at night.

"If you're going out anyway. But don't make a special trip for me."

Crawford snorted. "I've got about four hours of paperwork to get through tonight. Trust me, I'm going anyway. Possibly more than once."

Mateus winced internally. Crawford had been so amazing through all of this, never once getting angry about how much this marriage had inconvenienced him. Even now, staying in a second-rate motel with a nonfunctional coffeemaker, he didn't snap or try to make Mateus feel bad. Instead, he offered to pick up Mateus's new favorite evening drink while he went out to get coffee to fuel a late-night work session that was necessary because he'd spent all day doing things for Mateus.

"Do you want me to come with you?" Mateus didn't make a move to get up from the bed since he was reasonably sure the answer was going to be no. He and Crawford had been together literally all day, which meant Crawford probably needed a little alone time to recharge. He always got a bit tense and grumpy when he didn't have any time to himself.

He'd closed his eyes again, but he heard the rasp of Crawford swiping his keys off the bureau. "No, I'm good. I may take my laptop and take advantage of the Wi-Fi to finish up a report that needs to be sent in. The connection here is pretty crappy. But I'll be back in an hour or so with your coffee, okay?"

Mateus fought back a smile. "Okay. Thanks."

"Don't mention it," Crawford said. A moment later the door snicked shut behind him.

Mateus sat up and rubbed his eyes. He'd gotten better about not effusively thanking Crawford for helping him, but he knew even his routine and polite thank-yous made Crawford uncomfortable. He'd have to figure out a way to thank him without outright saying it.

Though how much longer would it be a problem? They'd see the immigration officer in the morning, and then Crawford would drop him off at the orchard. From what he'd read online, there might be another interview or two in the next year—once they got past the initial assessment and the ominous-sounding home visit—but it wouldn't be anything too invasive. And it probably wouldn't even be necessary, since by then Duarte would be able to hire Mateus and help him get a work visa.

The thought of not seeing Crawford every day made Mateus's stomach hurt. He'd let himself fall for Crawford even though he'd known it was a mistake. Crawford was clear about not wanting this to progress to an actual physical relationship, and Mateus accepted that. He had to. The ball was in Crawford's court, so to speak, and Crawford was content to let it sit. Mateus wasn't going to go against Crawford's wishes and try to pursue him. He owed Crawford a hell of a lot, and since Crawford seemed determined not to let Mateus repay him, the least he could do was respect the man's boundaries.

And oh, what boundaries he had. Mateus huffed out a laugh and rolled over, burying his face in the pillow. Life would be a lot easier right now if he could get past his obsession with Crawford's ass, but it was too magnificent to ignore. Then again, *without* Crawford's magnificent ass, Mateus's ass would be back in Portugal, or possibly in jail, right now. A little sexual frustration was a small price to pay for staying in the country.

If this had been a romantic comedy like the ones Bree had gotten him addicted to on Netflix, the room would ring with silence, and Mateus would sit and pine. But the walls were too thin for that, and instead his pity party was set to the soundtrack of a couple having a loud conversation about dinner next door. He wanted to try the diner they'd passed on the drive in, and she wanted to go to Applebee's. Mateus silently cheered the man on as he ranted about bland, overpriced chain restaurants.

Not that the diner was any better. He and Crawford had stopped there for dinner, and Mateus couldn't even remember what he'd ordered. But he agreed with the man on principle.

If he were back at the orchard, he'd be outside. Walking the fence line to make sure it was intact, checking on the trees he and Duarte had staked before he left, tinkering with an engine in the barn. Mateus hated being cooped up indoors. It hadn't been so bad in Vancouver, since he'd had his days free to roam around the city. It wasn't as nice as being out in nature, but it was better than being stuck inside.

There wasn't anywhere to escape to here since the motel was nestled into an office park. It was dark enough to make walking through dimly lit parking lots an unattractive option, even if he had wanted to explore the suburban concrete jungle.

A door slammed down the hall, and the arguing couple faded out of his hearing. The room still wasn't quiet, between a ticking clock on the far wall and the rattle of the ventilation system. If he strained he could hear cars on the highway that bordered the edge of the office park.

It wasn't a great setup for peaceful introspection, which was good because Mateus didn't think he'd like what he found if he did any serious soul-searching right now: a lot of pining after Crawford, and a fair amount of self-pity over the situation they were in. He didn't have much of a right to that, since it was entirely his own fault.

He should call Duarte and let him know he'd be coming home tomorrow, but at this point he wasn't sure if he'd be coming with Crawford or alone, so he was going to take the cowardly route and put the call off until tomorrow.

Would he be bringing Crawford home to the orchard? They hadn't talked about the disastrous revelations in the interrogation room. He felt stupid for not realizing there would be a home visit, but how could he have known? Duarte had never said anything about that after he'd married Bree. Crawford probably needed to get back to Los Angeles for work. And he definitely needed to be there soon or he'd miss seeing his nephew and sister-in-law off, and Mateus didn't want that on his conscience. Crawford had told him a lot about Brandon, and it was obvious he and Adam were an important part of Crawford's life. Mateus could handle a week or two in California if it meant Crawford got to resume his life.

On the other hand, he'd been gone long enough from the orchard that work was starting to pile up. The last time he'd talked to Bree, she'd sounded stressed, and he hated that. Maybe Duarte could take on a hired hand for a month or so.

Mateus groaned and buried his head under the pillow. Duarte couldn't afford to pay *him*; he definitely couldn't afford someone who would actually want to work for a real wage. He needed to get back to the orchard to pick up some of the slack or they'd be writing off another growing season.

He hated to ask Crawford for another favor, but it looked like that was going to have to happen. Though there was no reason to put the cart before the horse. Maybe Officer Suarez wouldn't need to do a home visit for a month or two. That would give him some time to get caught up at the orchard and then head down to Los Angeles for a few days.

MATEUS didn't remember drifting off, but the next thing he knew Crawford was shaking him awake. He blinked away the fuzziness in his vision, his mouth watering when he smelled rather than saw the coffee Crawford was holding out to him.

"You looked exhausted, but I didn't want you to fall asleep in your clothes and wake up a sweaty mess in the middle of the night. Plus you had the pillow over your face, and this bed is hard as a rock. You'd probably kill your neck sleeping like that."

Mateus sat up and leaned against the headboard before taking the coffee. It was perfect. No whipped cream, just like he liked it. It was still hot, too, so Crawford must have waited to order it until he'd been ready to leave Starbucks. The thoughtfulness of the gesture made Mateus's toes curl with homey satisfaction.

He stretched, his attention drawn to the way Crawford tracked his movements. Crawford's gaze lingered on the strip of skin that was exposed when Mateus's shirt rode up. He didn't tug it back down like he usually would. He liked having Crawford's attention on him, and while he wasn't going to force the issue and make things uncomfortable for Crawford, he also wasn't above playing a little dirty.

"Thanks for the coffee," he said, taking another slow sip. He didn't think he was imagining the way Crawford's breath quickened.

"Anytime." Crawford blinked and then pulled out his phone, cursing softly. "Shit. Time. It's time for me to Skype with Brandon, and he's already called twice. Do you mind? I can go out to the hallway if it would bother you."

Mateus waved off his concern. "It's fine. I can put on headphones if you want some privacy."

Crawford shook his head. "Actually, he'll probably want to see you. Do you mind? He was bummed he didn't get to meet you when we talked last week."

Mateus had been out meeting up with the friends he'd made on the walking tour. He'd been a little bummed to have missed it himself.

"If you're okay with me meeting him, I'd love to. He sounds like a great kid."

Crawford had already opened Skype on his phone and started dialing Brandon, and he burst out laughing as it started to ring. "Oh please, say that to him. He hates being called a kid. He thinks he's a man—it's hilarious."

Mateus scooted over to make room for Crawford, his thigh and arm tingling where they brushed up against Crawford's as Crawford got settled in against the headboard.

Crawford's screen filled with Brandon's image when he picked up. He was grinning ear to ear as he greeted his uncle, and Crawford was lit up just as much.

"Hey, miscreant. How have the last few days of school been going?"

Brandon rolled his eyes. "Mom's making me stay in until the day before we leave. Can you believe it?"

Crawford laughed. "Hey, it's extra time with your friends. And it's not like you're the one packing up the house, right?"

Brandon gave an indignant squeak. "I packed a little." He panned the camera around his room. There were a few suitcases, and one of them had a fluffy white tail hanging out of it.

"Are you trying to steal my cat?"

"Bub, get out!" A shoe came sailing from the direction of the camera and hit the box. The cat came scrambling out with a hiss and streaked out the bedroom door.

"That was Beelzebub," Crawford explained. "He's always liked Brandon more than me, though I have no idea why. I've never thrown a shoe at him."

Brandon turned the camera back on himself. “Slander,” he said. “Besides, you’ve thrown more than just shoes at him.”

Crawford tilted the camera and leaned in closer so both he and Mateus were in view. “Bran, this is Mateus. Mateus, this is my nephew Brandon.”

“Oh, hey man, nice to meet you! Are you coming to LA with Uncle Crawford? Dad said you two got married in Vancouver. That’s kind of wild, I’m not gonna lie.”

Mateus liked him already. “It’s nice to meet you too. And yes, your uncle and I did get married. But I don’t think I’m coming to LA anytime soon. My brother owns an orchard here in Washington, and there’s a lot to do with the trees this time of year.”

“That’s so cool. I totally want to visit when I’m home next summer. So,” he bit his lip, and the gesture made him look eerily similar to Crawford, “did Dad tell you I’m spending next summer with you, Uncle Crawford?”

Adam hadn’t, but Crawford didn’t mind. He’d love to have Brandon for the summer. “No, but I’m sure we can work it out.”

“Maybe I can get a summer job at the orchard. Will you be moving to Washington? I mean, since we’re not going to be in LA anymore, it’s not like you have to stay here, right?”

Crawford coughed and rubbed his neck. “Ah, we haven’t really discussed it yet. It was all kind of sudden.”

Brandon let out a guffaw. “Kind of sudden? Yeah, Uncle Crawford, you marrying someone you just met was *kind of sudden*. Jeez. And you wonder why I didn’t ask you for dating advice about the dance.” His cheeks dimpled when he smiled. “No offense, Mateus.”

“None taken. It was pretty fast. Your uncle’s an awesome guy, though. I’m lucky to have him.” It was the absolute truth. Crawford knocked his knee into Mateus's, and Mateus grinned. "He could learn to take a compliment, though. That's one of his shortfalls."

Brandon laughed again, his eyes shining as he looked at Crawford on the screen. Past the puppy fat that was melting away, Mateus could see that Brandon had the same strong jaw and nose that Crawford did. He was going to be a looker when he was older, just like his uncle. He'd bet that Adam was attractive too. The Hargrave genes must be pretty good.

Brandon's laughter died away, leaving the hint of a fond smile. "I'm just glad he's not going to be alone when we leave for Japan."

"Hey now, I'll have Bub," Crawford said.

"Yeah, and who's going to watch him when you travel? You're going to have to put him up in one of those fancy pet hotels or something. Does Chatham-Thompson have any of those? Maybe you'd get a discount."

"Gotta be cheaper than your rates, kid."

Brandon pursed his lips. "You pay me a pittance."

"I pay you plenty. Good word, though. SAT tutoring coming along?"

Brandon huffed out a sigh. "I tried to convince Dad that I didn't need to take them now that we'll be living in Japan, but that was a no-go."

"You'll do fine. And you do need to take them to get into college so you can get a good job."

Brandon's gaze shifted to Mateus. "Maybe I could work for your brother."

Mateus grinned. "Well, I have a masters in botany, and Duarte has his MBA. So I'd say you'd better make college plan A."

Brandon groaned. "I'm not sure I like you anymore."

Crawford snorted. "You'd better get to bed, kid. You have school in the morning. Give Bub an ear scratch for me, and tell your mom and dad I said hi."

"Will do. Are you going to be back before we go?"

Crawford looked over at Mateus and back at the screen. "I'll definitely be there, I just don't know for how long. Mateus and I have some things we have to sort out here, but I wouldn't miss your good-bye party. I promise."

Brandon bit his lip again. "You're just worried I'll take Beelzebub with me."

Crawford put a hand over his heart. "You caught me. Night, Bran. Love you lots, kiddo."

"Love you too, Uncle Crawford. Bye, Mateus."

Crawford dropped the phone on the bed when Brandon hung up and leaned heavily against the headboard, closing his eyes.

Mateus wanted to reach out and hug him, but he wasn't sure it would be welcome. "You're going to miss him a lot when he leaves."

"Tons. But we'll skype, and apparently he's spending the whole summer with me, so we'll get by." He opened his eyes and blew out a breath. "We'll have to work out where we're going to be for the home visits and how we're going to handle that, but I'm beat. Would you mind if we talked about it tomorrow?"

Mateus couldn't agree more. Running from a problem never solved anything, but postponing it wouldn't hurt.

"I don't mind." He looked down at the bed. "You can take the bed. I'll sleep on the love seat."

It was lumpy and it didn't pull out, but Crawford had taken the couch in Vancouver, so he deserved the bed here. It was probably only marginally more comfortable, anyway.

Crawford's hand shot out and closed around Mateus's wrist when he started to slide off the bed.

"We can share. There's no way a grown man can fit on that tiny sofa, and this bed is plenty big."

Mateus's pulse kicked up a notch at the thought of sleeping with Crawford, but from the exhausted slump to Crawford's shoulders, he could tell it was an invitation literally to do just that—sleep.

He should've said no.

Chapter Fourteen

CRAWFORD woke up on the wrong side of the bed—literally. He'd started out on his side, facing away from Mateus with as much space as physically possible between them. Crawford's muscles ached from keeping them tense as he clung to the edge of the mattress for the sleepless first half of the night.

Sometime during the night, though, his body had given up the fight and he'd drifted off, and now Crawford was face-to-face with a sleeping Mateus. Their legs were tangled, and Mateus had an arm slung over Crawford's shoulder. His fingers brushed against Crawford's back with each breath Crawford took, and that casual contact and the tickle of Mateus's leg hair against his own had Crawford going from groggy to wide-awake in record time.

Mateus looked peaceful and relaxed, and Crawford wished they could just stay in the crappy hotel bed forever. Thoughts like that were dangerous. He clearly needed to get up and put some distance between them.

Crawford swallowed and pushed his way gently out of Mateus's light hold. He rolled to the side and climbed out of the bed carefully, though not much could be done about the creak and pop of the flimsy bed's springs. It was a relief to make it to the bathroom where he couldn't see Mateus's stupidly perfect sleeping face. All the walls Crawford had tried to build had come crashing down the moment he'd woken up close enough to count Mateus's eyelashes. There was nothing casual about waking up with their breath mingling and their bodies intertwined, no matter how innocent the pose was.

It was exactly the kind of memory Crawford didn't want to have. It felt proprietary, when nothing could be further from the truth. He didn't have any claim to Mateus, and he couldn't do anything about the fact that Mateus undeniably had claim over him, despite Crawford's best efforts to keep his distance.

It was ridiculously early, but Crawford didn't like his chances of getting back to sleep. He slipped into the shower to wash away the aches and cricks from his night of restless sleep. If Mateus was still asleep when he got out, he'd run down to the Starbucks for breakfast. If they got moving early, they could be first in line to see Officer Suarez. As much as he dreaded the end of his time with Mateus, Crawford needed a plan. He hated not knowing what was going to happen next, and right now everything was a big question mark.

The cheap hotel towels were scratchy and thin, but they smelled reassuringly of bleach, which at least meant they were clean. He'd been in and out of a lot of hotel rooms in his career, and even though this one wasn't fancy, it was well-kept and sanitary. That was more than he could say for a lot of the high-end places he'd been, so he tried to tamp down on his inner snob as he wrapped the towel around his waist and stepped out into the room. It had been important to Mateus that he be the one to pay for the room, and Crawford respected that too much to complain about the rough sheets and lack of amenities.

Mateus was already sitting up, the blankets pooled around his waist and his hair sleep-mussed and tangled.

"It's early," he murmured, his voice hoarse.

"You can go back to sleep. I was going to run out and get us something to eat."

Mateus perked up. "And some coffee?"

"No, I thought this might be a good day to quit caffeine cold-turkey."

Mateus groaned and fell back onto the mattress. "It's early."

Crawford snickered. Mateus was definitely not a morning person. Somehow he managed to make it endearing. "You've said. Go back to sleep. I'll wake you up when I'm back with breakfast."

CRAWFORD clutched his second latte of the day like a lifeline, still shell-shocked over their meeting with Officer Suarez. Surprisingly, he and Mateus had done well on the initial questionnaire. It helped that neither of them had a large family, so those questions were easy.

It had been a lot less *Newlywed Game* and a lot more standardized test than Crawford had envisioned.

Maybe if they'd blown that part of it Officer Suarez wouldn't have been so eager to set up a home visit immediately.

"Should we have told her we were going to be at your place in LA? Maybe that would have delayed things. She'd have to find someone down there to do the home visit then, right? We could call her back—"

Crawford shook his head. "My place is—well, it's kind of empty. I haven't really gotten around to doing any decorating, since I'm rarely there."

"We have two weeks. You could go back to LA and come up a day or two before the visit," Mateus offered weakly.

He didn't sound convinced, even though it was his idea. "That's what I figured we'd do. Is that a problem?"

Mateus winced. "Not exactly? Except. Yes. My brother, he's—" He broke off and stared down at the table for a moment. "He's *antiquado*. Old-school. Marriage is sacred to him, and he'd be angry we were dishonoring the rite the way we are.

"Duarte is progressive on his view of sexuality, but he's as Catholic as can be when it comes to marriage being a sacrament. He'd never forgive me for marrying you just for a green card. We're going to have to lie to him."

Crawford found himself grinning at the prospect of continuing their sham of a marriage, which was bizarre. He just couldn't help but feel at ease around Mateus, though, and the thought of meeting his family and seeing the orchard Mateus had talked so glowingly about was undeniably appealing. Even if it did mean forcing Mateus to be dishonest with them.

"I—does that bother you? We're too far in to go back, but we could come clean to the immigration agent and hire a lawyer for us. We could fight the deportation."

Mateus laughed. "Crawford. Really? There's no chance of that working. That's the whole point of the home visit. If they found out our marriage was fake, I'd be arrested on the spot. So would you."

"Well, we could keep it up for the visit, and then you could tell your brother we fought and are taking some time apart. Have a long separation and then divorce after he's able to hire you, and if immigration had a problem, you could get a work visa then."

Mateus pursed his lips. "There is absolutely zero chance of my family buying that story. They know me too well. You're exactly my type. I wouldn't let someone like you just walk away, especially not if I'd loved you enough to marry you."

Crawford's throat tightened. "You'd fight for me?"

Mateus seemed to realize what he'd said a second later. His face crumpled with concern, and he reached out and grabbed Crawford's free hand. "Without question. You're an amazing man, Crawford. And Davis was an asshole for leaving you. I'm sorry."

Crawford looked away, uncomfortable with the swell of emotion he felt. He took another drink of the latte he hadn't really even wanted, but had ordered just to have something to hold.

"Officer Suarez is coming in almost two weeks. I need to see Brandon before he leaves, and I want to get back to spend time with Adam before he goes, but I can do that afterward." He looked up at Mateus. "Man, I wish there was time to bring Brandon to the orchard. I really think he'd love it."

"He's welcome. Your whole family is. Duarte and Bree would be thrilled to have them."

Crawford shook his head with a frown. "There's too much to do before they leave. I promised him I'd come back for his party, but I can fly down for just a day. It's this weekend, so it won't interfere with the home visit."

"Even if it did, Brandon's more important. You need to be there for that."

"I didn't exactly pack for manual labor, so maybe we could pick up some things while we're in the city? Just to tide me over till I can get home this weekend and get some fresh clothes."

Mateus's eyes widened. "I'm not bringing you to the orchard to work!"

"Why the hell not? From what you've said, there's plenty to do. I've already taken the week off, and depending on what comes up I may take next week off too. I'm not claiming to have a green thumb, but I can be a good grunt. Surely there's some unskilled labor for me."

"We can find something for you, but it's really not necessary."

"I insist. Maybe we can stop and grab some basics on the way to Beverly."

Mateus released his hand and sat back. "I can call Duarte and have him come get us. It's about two hours to Beverly."

"We could rent a car—"

Mateus glared at him. "No. There's nowhere to return one there, anyway. We'll have Duarte come. Bree will probably want to come with him and do a little shopping here. It's fine."

Crawford bumped his knee against Mateus's under the table. "You could do some of that sightseeing you talked about. It would be a shame to waste a day in Seattle."

Crawford would have preferred to rent a car to have out at the orchard, but he didn't want to press the issue. The beaming smile he got from Mateus was worth a day of wandering around the city.

Mateus's grin faded when Crawford's phone rang on the table between them. Davis's name was on the caller ID. "You should get that. Work is more important than letting me play tourist. I'll call Duarte and figure out a plan for where they can pick us up. I can't apologize enough for how complicated this has become. I never wanted you to be this put out."

Crawford sent the call to voice mail. "I'm on vacation this week. There's nothing that could be happening that's so important it can't wait a few hours while we go see Pike Place Market and maybe feed some sea lions." He was surprised to find he actually meant it.

"As for this being complicated—life is complicated. And it was my lie that got us into this, so if it's anyone's fault, it's mine. But I'd do it again with no regrets. You deserve to be happy. And if being here and working with your brother in the orchard is what makes you happy, then I'm going to do everything I can to make sure you get to do that."

He nudged Mateus's knee again. "Besides, I'd really like to see the orchard that has you willing to risk deportation and jail," Crawford said, surprising himself yet again with the truth of the statement. By rights, he should have been desperate to get through the next two weeks as quickly as possible so he could go home and put this whole ordeal behind him, but something about

Mateus was calming, despite the fact that he so often left Crawford confused.

Mateus blew out a breath and nodded slowly. "Okay. Yes. Okay," he murmured, and Crawford wondered if it was more Mateus reassuring himself than anything else. "I'll call Duarte. And we'll need to do something with our bags."

Crawford rolled his eyes. "There are four Chatham-Thompson properties in Seattle, including one about a quarter of a mile from Pike Place. We can leave them there till we're ready to go."

Mateus pulled his phone out of his pocket and stood up. "Just so you know," he said conversationally as he started to dial, "my sister-in-law is going to eat you alive."

Chapter Fifteen

MATEUS was tired, but it was a good tired. The kind of achiness that came from spending hours walking around a big city taking in the sights. Just as he'd predicted, Bree had wanted to do a little shopping, and then Crawford had treated the four of them to dinner. It had been almost nine by the time they'd pulled up to the farmhouse, too dark to show Crawford the orchard.

They'd taken up residence at the kitchen table with a bottle of wine instead, and Mateus had been pleasantly surprised by how well Duarte and Crawford were getting along.

Just like he'd thought, Bree had taken to Crawford immediately. She'd also noticed their wedding bands about thirty seconds after she and Duarte had gotten out of the car—and that had been a scene. It was so romantic, she'd said. Like a fairy tale.

That was exactly what this was like. But not the sanitized Disney versions. This was a Grimm's fairy tale in the making, and Mateus was going to be the one who ended up in pieces at the end.

He didn't even realize how late it had gotten until he looked up and saw that Bree's chair was empty.

"She went up to bed an hour ago," Duarte said. He held a half-full bottle of wine up in question, but Mateus shook his head. He was too muzzy. Besides, he didn't remember Duarte opening the third bottle at all. But he must have, because two empties now lined the table. "She'd never admit it, but the pregnancy makes her tired."

"Growing a person is hard work," Crawford said, nodding.

Mateus laughed. He put his hand over his glass when Duarte let the bottle hover over it. "I've had enough, and I think Crawford has too. We should get to bed, and you should get back to your lovely wife before she comes down and skins us all alive for getting drunk when she can't."

"True, true," Duarte murmured.

It was well past midnight when they finally made it back to Mateus's room, stumbling inside with drunken laughs and unsteady steps thanks to the excellent wine Duarte had insisted on opening in celebration of their elopement. He seemed to agree with Bree that fate and happy coincidence had brought them together, which was true, in a way.

"I can't believe you told your brother that I giggled when we kissed in front of the customs agent," Crawford said, picking up the thread of a conversation from hours earlier.

"You can't deny it, Crawford. I was there," Mateus said, eyebrows winging up dramatically. "You giggled."

Crawford blushed. "It was an act, Mateus. Just like those little kittenish moans of yours were," he said, smiling triumphantly when Mateus's cheeks darkened and he looked away.

"One, I did not moan. And two, I bet I could make you do it again," Mateus said, his voice husky.

"I bet I could make *you* do it again," Crawford answered, arching a brow when Mateus stepped into his space, their bodies barely touching. "That would prove you did it in the first place."

"Fine, then."

"Fine."

Crawford's mouth was on his before Mateus could fully digest the challenge. His heart was racing as his mind caught up to his mouth, his thoughts muddled by the wine and Crawford's intoxicating scent.

Mateus wasn't going to back down. He closed the tiny gap between them, bringing his hand up to cup the back of Crawford's head as he brought their lips together. Crawford tasted of wine and some undefinable spice that seemed to make Mateus lose all rational thought. He crowded against Crawford, licking into his mouth with strong, bold strokes, his other hand coming up to cradle Crawford's jaw, his touch light and reverent.

Mateus couldn't hold back a soft moan. Crawford hummed triumphantly, but before he could pull away and claim victory, Mateus wrapped his arms around him and kept him close, deepening the kiss.

Crawford stumbled and hit the wall behind them hard enough to make the picture frames rattle. Part of Mateus's brain was screaming at him to stop, but he couldn't seem to remember why kissing Crawford was a bad idea. Kissing Crawford was brilliant, and clearly, he should never stop.

When Crawford's hips pressed against his own, Mateus moaned again, a pang of pure need singing through him as he felt how much Crawford wanted him. He shifted his hips slightly and was rewarded by a groan from Crawford. He carded his hand through Crawford's hair, fingers rubbing against his scalp as he tried to draw him in even closer.

He canted his hips forward again, but this time instead of returning the pressure, Crawford pulled away.

"So it's a draw, then," Crawford said breathlessly, and Mateus blinked, confused.

"I giggled, you moaned, we're even," Crawford explained, and Mateus belatedly remembered the bet that had prompted their runaway kissing session.

"Right," he said, swallowing hard. What was he doing? Kissing Crawford when they'd both been drinking had been a mistake.

Crawford cleared his throat, making Mateus feel even more awkward. He always managed to be at loose ends around Crawford.

"So are we both sleeping in here?"

Mateus followed his gaze to the queen-size bed that had felt perfectly adequate up until now. The bed they'd shared last night had been larger, but this one should work.

"It would be weird if we didn't. There's a guest room, but this is an old house." Mateus shifted, making the floorboards squeak. "You can't get anywhere without the whole house knowing."

Crawford didn't seem too upset by the prospect. "Do you want the bathroom first or second?"

He wanted to go first so there was at least a chance he might be asleep by the time Crawford slid into bed with him, but that was a slim chance. “You go ahead. I’m going to get some clean sheets on the bed for us.”

Bree met him in the hallway, still wearing her makeup from earlier. It had smudged when she’d fallen asleep, and it made her look like a sad panda. Not that he was going to tell her that.

“Do you need anything?”

He didn’t know why she bothered whispering. Crawford was in the bathroom down the hall with the water running, and Duarte slept like the dead.

“No. Did we wake you?”

“The baby woke me,” she said with a grimace. “I have to pee every five minutes, I swear.”

“I’m just getting clean sheets. You should go back to bed.”

She nodded sleepily. “I will. I just wanted to give you these,” she said, pressing a box into his hand.

He looked down, squinting in the moonlight as he tried to make out what was written on it. Mortification bloomed as soon as he did. “Condoms? Bree!”

“Well, it’s not like Duarte and I need them right now. Someone may as well get some use out of them.”

“Bree,” he whined.

She grinned. “Have a good night,” she sang. She blew him a kiss before disappearing back into her bedroom, closing the door behind herself.

He looked down at the open box of condoms he was holding, wishing he could take back the last minute. He’d stay in his room and they’d sleep on musty sheets. It would have been preferable to what had just happened.

He shoved the condoms to the back of the linen closet when he heard the bathroom door open. Who knew what Crawford would do if he saw them. Probably accuse Mateus of planning to seduce him. Not that Mateus wouldn't love to, but he wasn't going to make a move unless Crawford stopped running so hot and cold. The mixed signals were killing him.

He gathered up fresh sheets and made his way back to the bedroom, cursing Bree all the way for putting images he didn't need in his head.

IT was a little disconcerting how well Crawford melted into their daily routine. He couldn't tell a weed from an herb, which made him useless in the garden, but he was more than capable of hauling away branches and other debris and patching fences.

Mateus's resolve not to jump him was waning every day. It was hard to remain resolute when faced with the sight of a shirtless Crawford sweating in the sun as he lifted hay bales and moved hundred-pound bags of fertilizer. The man had more muscle than any desk jockey had a right to, and it was driving Mateus crazy.

Not that the nights were any better. They were worse—far worse. After the second morning waking up spooned together in Mateus's bed, they'd given up all pretense of not cuddling. Last night Crawford had snuggled right up to him the moment they'd climbed between the sheets, and it hadn't felt platonic in the least.

Not that they'd talked about it. Mateus didn't want to push, not when Crawford was finally starting to loosen up around him. But he wanted a hell of a lot more than mutual cuddling with Crawford. He just didn't know how to get to that point without scaring him away.

Mateus held his hand up to shield his eyes from the sun as he looked down the row of Cameo trees he'd been staking. The storm the night before had done some damage, and Mateus was out doing what he could to mitigate it. From where he was, he could see Crawford repairing a fence in the far field.

He looked just as at-home with a hammer in his hand as he had with his laptop and spreadsheets. There didn't seem to be much Crawford couldn't do. Bree's morning sickness had become all-day sickness, and last night Crawford had even stepped in and made dinner. He was so perfect it hurt. Mateus was already mourning the loss of his company, and he still had him here for another week.

"You'd better go shower," he yelled, cupping his hands around his mouth. "Duarte's taking you to the airport in an hour!"

Crawford was flying back to LA for Brandon's going-away party. He'd complained about being the only one Brandon invited who was old enough to vote, but Mateus knew he was happy to be there for him. He'd only be gone a day and a half, but it would be good to get a break from each other. Maybe it would give Mateus a chance to gain some perspective.

He watched as Crawford finished the rail he was working on and wiped his hands on his jeans. He wasn't close enough to fully appreciate how the movement pulled the fabric taut across his ass, but he was blessed—or maybe in this case cursed—with a fabulous imagination.

Crawford jogged toward him, cradling the toolbox against his chest. "There's a tree two rows over that snapped in the wind last night," he said as he approached.

Mateus sighed. There wasn't much he could do if the trunk had actually snapped. "I'll take care of it. Thanks for working on the fence. Duarte's been trying to get to that for weeks. The neighbor has cows that get into the orchard sometimes."

Crawford grinned. "That I'd like to see."

They'd spent three hours herding them back to the fence last time. "Trust me, it's less fun than you'd think."

He felt his back pocket, pulling out Crawford's phone. "You left this in the barn. It's been buzzing on and off for the last hour."

Crawford made a face and scrolled through his messages. He sucked in a sharp breath. "Son of a bitch," he muttered.

His eyes flashed when he looked up, his jaw tight. All the easy relaxation from a minute earlier was gone. "George needs to talk to me. He's got another assignment for me. He wants Davis and me to work together on a hotel that's struggling in Brussels, since we did such a good job in Vancouver."

Mateus's stomach dropped. It wasn't like he hadn't known Crawford would go back to his real life and his job, but hearing about it in stark terms made it a lot more real. Especially since it meant throwing Crawford back in with Davis. "Do you have to?"

Crawford's lips were a grim, bloodless line. "No, I don't. And I'm going to make it clear to George that if working with Davis is going to become a regular thing, he can take this job and shove it up his pompous ass."

"You don't mean that. You're angry, but you don't want to quit."

The tension bled out of Crawford's shoulders. "Actually, I do. I haven't been happy there for a long time, and if this is going to be how he rewards me for years of hard work, then I don't want to work for him anymore."

A thrill went up Mateus's spine at the thought of Crawford quitting. It was ridiculous; of course Crawford leaving his job didn't mean he'd move to Beverly. He'd get another job and probably move even farther away. But Mateus couldn't help but be a little giddy at the prospect.

The bubbly, happy feeling was at odds with the niggle of guilt that sat heavy in his stomach, though. He was responsible for uprooting Crawford's life. It seemed like Crawford was happy about it now, but would he still be in a week? A month?

"I'm going to go shower and call George. I'll see you Sunday," Crawford said. He hesitated, and then stepped forward and pressed a soft kiss to Mateus's cheek. "Thanks."

Chapter Sixteen

CRAWFORD had insisted on renting a car when he came back from LA, and after two round-trips to Seattle in less than a week, Duarte hadn't argued. Crawford hadn't splurged on a fancy car this time because he didn't know how long he'd have it. He hadn't booked a flight back to LA yet either. He had all the time in the world, now that he didn't have a job to get back to.

It had been cathartic to hand in his letter of resignation. He'd gone in on Sunday before heading to the airport, and George had been there to try to talk him out of it. He hadn't backed down from his insistence that Crawford work with Davis again, and if Crawford was being honest with himself—something he had promised himself he was going to do more often—he was glad. It was a relief to leave Chatham-Thompson, even though he'd built a successful career there over almost two decades. He was ready to move on and try something different.

Mateus had been oddly distant since Crawford's return, but it wasn't until Crawford accidentally eavesdropped on a conversation between Mateus and Bree that he figured out why. They'd been outside the open window arguing when Crawford walked into the kitchen to grab a drink.

"—you happy about this?"

Bree's tone was muted but sharp, and it had caught Crawford's attention before he'd even realized Mateus was also there.

"I am." Mateus sounded miserable for someone claiming to be happy. "But it's fast, Bree. What if he wakes up tomorrow and regrets it? What if he ends up blaming me for quitting? I don't want to be the reason he gave up his career."

Crawford had slunk back into the living room without his drink, feeling awkward. Mateus had voiced that fear before Crawford had quit, though not in quite such blunt terms. Was that why he'd been so reserved? He was waiting for the other shoe to drop, afraid Crawford would regret quitting his job and blame it on Mateus? This was a good change. A sudden one, sure. But it was for the best. Crawford hadn't felt this free in years. It was ironic, but he felt like his life had more direction than it had in a long time, even though he didn't know where he was going. He'd tried to express that, but Crawford was afraid he had fallen short.

When Bree and Mateus came back inside a few minutes later, Bree had shoved Mateus into the living room to sit in an awkward, polite silence with Crawford, and gone to work in the kitchen.

"I—you know this was a long time coming, right? I wasn't happy being an internal auditor." Crawford wasn't sure how to broach the subject without making it obvious he'd been listening to their conversation. "You gave me the courage to finally quit, and I owe you a huge thank-you for that."

Mateus looked up and fully met his gaze for the first time since he'd gotten back from LA. "You don't think it's just you reacting to all the stress?"

Crawford grinned. "Are you kidding? This is the least amount of stress I've been under in months. Maybe years. Mateus, this is a good thing."

Bree appeared in the archway to the kitchen, holding a gigantic wicker basket. "See, Mat? Crawford is happy about leaving his job," she said, emphasizing the word happy and giving Mateus a significant look. She held the basket out. "I made you lunch. Go celebrate."

Mateus stepped forward to take the overburdened basket. "You didn't need to do that. I could have made us lunch."

She waved him off. "I didn't have to do it, but I did. I'm happy to. Go show him how beautiful the orchard is, Mateus. Give him a reason to stay here now that he isn't tied to LA!"

They'd walked a fair bit, through the orchard and out into land far enough away that Crawford didn't know whether it was still Duarte's. Mateus hadn't been worried, so Crawford figured the neighbors must be friendly. They'd stayed out of the pasture with the cows, but other than that, they'd just wandered without a clear plan.

It had been nice, at least up until a few minutes ago when they'd chosen a spot to eat and the skies promptly opened up over them.

The rain pattered down around them, fat drops splashing against Crawford's skin and soaking into the quilt Bree had put in the basket.

"We should pack this up," Mateus said, casting a worried glance to the west. "I think it's going to get worse before it gets better."

The warm rain wasn't a problem, but the dark clouds and occasional lightning flashes a few miles in the distance spelled trouble. Crawford agreed with Mateus—he didn't want to be caught out in a pasture with a thunderstorm closing in.

Mateus was already on his knees gathering up their uneaten picnic. Crawford stood and waited until he'd gotten all the food before starting to fold up the blanket, scooping it up off the ground as soon as Mateus finished his task and stood as well.

A huge clap of thunder rolled above, loud enough that Crawford felt it reverberate in his chest. The storm was closer than he'd thought. "Should we make a run back to the house?"

Mateus shook his head, wiping wet hair out of his face. "We won't make it. We could try to find some shelter in the orchard, but I don't know if we should be under trees. We might do better going that way," he said, pointing off toward the other end of the clearing. The trees there were taller and denser.

Lighting scissored through the sky, and moments later the gentle rain became a downpour. "Better than standing here," Crawford yelled over the pounding rain. He folded the blanket in close to his body and took off toward the copse of trees after making sure Mateus was right behind him.

The canopy of leaves kept off the worst of the rain, but the lightning was still worrisome. Crawford dug his phone out of his pocket once they were both safely under the trees. No service.

"I can't pull up a radar," he said, showing Mateus the screen. "Should we stay here or try to find a barn or something on the property?"

Mateus squinted out into the rain. "Duarte's property ends there," he said, nodding toward the split-rail fence they'd climbed over when they'd stopped in the meadow. "I don't know what's out here. But there isn't anything on Duarte's land that could be a shelter other than the barn by the house."

Crawford was certain Mateus knew Duarte's property at least as well as Duarte himself, if not better. If he said there weren't any shelters, then there weren't any. "Should we explore on this side, then? Is this an orchard too?"

Mateus shook his head. "Just land, I think. No fields, just a wooded lot. Duarte said there was a house somewhere, but I've never seen it. It must be back pretty far from the road."

Thunder boomed, close enough to rattle Crawford's teeth. A house sounded pretty damn nice right about now. "Maybe the owners would let us hang out there until the storm passes."

"It's empty," Mateus said, his brows furrowed. "Has been since Duarte and Bree bought their place. But maybe there's a barn or shed that's unlocked."

Crawford was soaked to the skin, and while the rain had felt warm coming down, he was well on his way to being chilled now. Mateus was shivering, clutching the basket to himself like it could warm him. They had no way of figuring out how long the rain would last or if the storm would worsen. They needed to try to find shelter, even if it was just the covered porch of an abandoned house.

Wiping his sleeve across his face to dispel some of the droplets that were streaming from his hair and impairing his vision, Crawford asked, “Which way do you think we should head?”

Mateus looked around. “North.” He spun in a half circle and cocked his head. “This way,” he said after a moment, inclining his head deeper into the trees.

Their situation should have been enough to keep Crawford’s libido under control, but he felt a pulse of arousal at the easy way Mateus had been able to figure out which way to head. Who knew orienteering was a kink of his? Maybe it was a good thing he hadn’t joined the Boy Scouts with Adam. That could have made for some awkward camp-outs.

“Lead on,” he said, biting back a smile as he followed Mateus through the trees. There wasn’t a path, but the foliage wasn’t too heavy, though they had to climb over more than a few mossy tree trunks where trees had fallen and been swallowed up by the forest around them.

It was still raining, but they were protected enough that only a few drops were leaking through the canopy overhead. The trees also blocked out their view of the darkening sky, for the most part. What he could see through the gaps wasn’t encouraging. The sky was nearly black, and the thunder was much more frequent. The storm was almost directly above them, and Crawford hoped they would be able to find shelter soon.

Rain pelted him, and he blinked, realizing the trees were getting less dense. That meant they were providing less protection, but it also meant they might be coming up to a clearing. He hoped it was the farmhouse Mateus had been talking about.

Mateus drew up short, and Crawford almost crashed into the back of him, skidding on the wet leaves. He hooted when he saw what had caught Mateus's attention—it was the house. It was gorgeous, and not just because it looked like a lifesaver right now. It had dormers and garrets that made it look like something out of a fairy tale, right down to the low fieldstone fence that ran around its perimeter. The porch had an overhang that looked inviting, but the wind had picked up and the rain was coming in horizontally, pelting against the house's windows and soaking the whitewashed floorboards. It wouldn't provide them with much protection from the rain, but it should shelter them from the lightning.

Mateus grabbed his elbow and pulled him farther toward the edge of the trees. "There's a barn," he said, pointing toward the east. It was about 500 yards from the house, but it looked structurally sound, which was all Crawford cared about.

They'd made it a few steps before the rain stopped and the sky lightened. It turned a sickly green, which wasn't something Crawford had ever seen before. Apparently Mateus had, because he looped the picnic basket through one arm and reached back with another, grabbing on to Crawford's hand and tugging him forward as he broke into a flat-out run. "Hurry!" he yelled, tucking his head down.

Crawford couldn't even get out a question before he felt something sting the back of his neck. Once, twice, and then suddenly there was a deluge, too many to count, sharp pricks battering him all over. He ducked his head like Mateus, then used his free hand to unfurl the blanket, making a shelter for them. He shook free of Mateus's grip and held it up over them as best he could as they ran. The ground around them was littered with tiny pieces of hail. They didn't look bigger than peas, but they'd felt like boulders when they hit his skin. The blanket didn't keep them all off, but it was better than just being completely unprotected.

"Do you think it's locked?" he yelled as they neared the white clapboard barn.

"Probably not," Mateus yelled back. "These pole barns have to be padlocked, and I don't see one."

Crawford had no idea what a pole barn was, but he vowed to read up on barns and become an expert if they made it through this intact. They stumbled to a clumsy stop in front of the huge barn doors, and he sighed in relief when he realized they were closed with a large piece of timber. There was a spot for a lock, it looked like, but nothing was there.

Mateus hefted the large bar up, and the barn doors creaked open. They rushed inside, but Mateus didn't close the door behind them. There weren't any windows in the barn, and closing the door would plunge them into darkness.

Crawford let the blanket drop with a breathless laugh. "Oh my God," he panted.

Mateus took one look at him and started to laugh. He put the picnic basket down at his feet and closed the distance between them, his hands coming up to pluck at Crawford's hair. Crawford started to laugh when he realized he had hail in his hair. Mateus did too. It felt natural to return the favor, his fingers skating through Mateus's dark locks as he swept the melting ice out of it.

Crawford's heart was pounding from their run, and it sounded unnaturally loud in his own ears in the heavy silence of the deserted barn. He and Mateus were standing close enough that their breath mingled, and Crawford couldn't stop himself from stepping closer, near enough that he could count the drops of water in Mateus's eyelashes.

He hesitated, hovering within kissing distance until Mateus closed his eyes and leaned in the rest of the way, collapsing the small gap between them. He tasted like rain, wild and earthy. Electric, like the lightning that had chased them into this musty barn. Crawford pressed in, chasing the flavor across Mateus's lips and into his mouth when Mateus melted into the kiss and let him in.

Crawford's hands fisted in Mateus's wet sweater, pulling at it until Mateus backed away and took it off with one swift motion. He tossed it onto a bale of hay in the corner, and Crawford scrambled to take his own shirt off. The buttons were a challenge for his rain-chilled hands, but Mateus swooped in to help, and the two of them managed to wrest the stiff, wet fabric out of the way.

Crawford shivered once his skin was exposed, but when Mateus crowded in against him a moment later, the chill disappeared. Skin to skin, heat flared between them. Crawford ran his hands up and down Mateus's back, his fingers greedy for any part of him he could touch. He'd wanted to do this for weeks, and he wasn't about to waste any time now that he had Mateus bare in front of him.

He groaned when Mateus's lips left his, a thrill running through him when a second later Mateus latched on to his neck, licking and mouthing softly, leaving a trail of tingling skin in his wake. They'd kissed in the airport office a week ago, but it hadn't been like this. Mateus seemed to know exactly what buttons to push.

This time when Crawford shivered it had nothing to do with being cold and wet. He was coming apart under Mateus's hands, and they'd barely gotten started.

He tamped down hard on the part of his brain that told him none of his objections had been addressed. Things were no different than they had been when he'd put the brakes on two weeks ago, except this time he didn't have the willpower to walk away.

Mateus seemed on board, if the way he'd plastered himself to Crawford was any indication. But Crawford wasn't going to be satisfied with just a few kisses this time, and he needed to know that Mateus felt the same way.

"I have to—God," Crawford gasped as Mateus palmed him through his jeans. "Jesus, wait. Wait, Mateus. Stop."

Mateus stepped away, breathing hard. There was just enough light coming in from a window in the hayloft to set his eyes sparkling. They looked dark and full of want, but Crawford had to be sure.

"I want you," Crawford rasped out. "God, I want you. I've wanted you since I saw you in the airport. I just—I have to be sure. Do you want this? Not out of any sense of obligation, but actually want this?"

Mateus threw back his head and laughed. The sound echoed through the barn, drowning out the constant thrum of the rain against the roof. "There isn't anything I want more right now. I swear." He stepped forward, coming in close again. "You're the most frustrating, oblivious, stubborn, beautiful, amazing man." Mateus was toe to toe with him now, their gazes locked. "And I want any part of you you'll let me have."

Crawford's knees nearly buckled with relief. "Thank God," he muttered. He took more care this time, now that he knew he was allowed to touch.

Their kisses before had all been stolen moments, and Crawford meant to savor what was coming next. He couldn't do half the things he wanted to with Mateus here in this barn, but Crawford wasn't going to let that stop him.

He tried to tug Mateus down onto the hay, but Mateus pulled back, shaking his head. "You are so clearly a city boy," Mateus said with a laugh. He grabbed the discarded blanket and spread it over the pile. "Trust me, there are places you don't want hay."

Crawford's pulse spiked at the insinuation. When Mateus started to unbutton his jeans, Crawford snapped to attention, frantically tearing at his own. They were both soaking wet, which made the process more comedic than sexy, but it hardly mattered. When they had both struggled out of their clothes, Mateus lowered himself down onto the blanket and reached his hands out for Crawford, inviting him down as well.

He blanketed himself over Mateus, hungry for all the skin-to-skin contact he could get. Mateus didn't seem to mind. He laughed softly and then drew Crawford in for a kiss that had Crawford's toes curling.

Crawford couldn't help but start to rut against Mateus's hip, his breath catching every time Mateus's cock brushed against his own belly. Mateus made a frustrated noise and rolled them to the side. He rutted against Crawford's cock, and pleasure spiked through Crawford, leaving him feeling like he couldn't draw in enough air. It wasn't enough, though, so he licked his palm and wrapped both of their lengths in his grip, teasing the most beautiful sounds out of Mateus's mouth as he stroked them.

Mateus ran a hand down Crawford's side, urging his pelvis closer as he rutted up into Crawford's hand.

Between the friction against Crawford's cock and the delicious sounds Mateus was making, Crawford could barely hold himself back. He tightened his grip on the two of them, and Mateus groaned, canting his hips forward in tiny thrusts as he came. Crawford wasn't far behind, Mateus's come easing the way and letting him stroke himself harder and faster until he spilled over his fist, his come mixing with Mateus's.

Mateus pressed in closer, licking lazily into Crawford's mouth as the two of them regained their breath. Crawford had worked up a sweat, and now it was cooling on his skin. He shivered, and Mateus soothed him with another soft kiss as he drew up the sides of the blanket around them like a cocoon.

Mateus snuggled into his side, laying his head on Crawford's chest. The rain was still beating down, loud in the silence of the barn now that their breathing had returned to normal. Crawford felt like he should say something, but he didn't want to break the magic of the moment. He was truly content for the first time in a long time, and he didn't want to risk losing that.

Mateus seemed content to just lie there, and Crawford took his cues from him, staying still until his arm had fallen asleep and his foot started to cramp. The rain had stopped a bit ago, and even though he was loath to leave their little nest, it would be smart to get back to the house in case it was just a break in the storm.

"We should get back," Mateus said. He sat up and brushed hay out of his hair. "Duarte and Bree will be worried."

Crawford didn't know what to make of that, so he concentrated on getting into his wet clothes.

Chapter Seventeen

IT was still overcast when they emerged from the barn, but even the low light felt bright after the darkness indoors. Mateus blinked, trying to adjust to the sudden change, while Crawford closed up the barn behind them.

Mateus wandered up the gravel drive toward the house. Lace curtains hung in the windows, but they were open enough to allow him to peer inside. He could see a large stone fireplace, gleaming hardwood floors, and doilies on every flat surface. The furniture was dated and worn, but the place looked fairly well-kept.

"Who owns this?" Crawford asked when he joined Mateus on the porch.

"I don't know. I just know it's for sale. It was a boarding house, I think. Back in the forties. Duarte told me about it a while back."

There was a Realtor's lockbox on the front door, and Crawford took out his phone and entered the number into his address book.

"Are you interested in this house?" Mateus asked, incredulous.

"I'd like to get a closer look."

Mateus tried not to let his hopes run away with him. Crawford hadn't made him any promises. He'd been clear in the barn that he wanted Mateus, and that had been enough for Mateus at the time. But they hadn't exactly traded sweet nothings in the hay. They'd had sex. Hot, frantic, no-holds-barred sex. And now Mateus had no idea where that left them.

Except Crawford was looking at a house in Beverly.

That had to mean something, didn't it?

Crawford was pacing along the porch, his footfalls soft against the faded planks. "This has a lot of potential, don't you think? From what I can see, the bones of the house look pretty good. I'd replace this door with a nice set of french doors, and they'd open into a sitting room with overstuffed chairs and antique floor lamps for reading. And I'd keep a fire going there, even in the summer."

Mateus tried to see what Crawford did, but he didn't have the vision for it. Crawford bit his lip, his expression intent as he looked in every window he could reach from the porch.

"I bet the kitchen is really outdated, but I'd need to update it with commercial appliances anyway. I'd have to serve food, being this far out. It's not like there are a bunch of restaurants in town, right?"

Mateus shook his head dumbly. "There's not much of a town, really. What exactly are you thinking? I'm lost."

Crawford's entire face lit up. "A bed-and-breakfast."

Mateus looked around. The place was pretty, sure. But it wasn't like Beverly was a tourist destination.

"It's every hipster's wet dream out here. Lots of land, an old farmhouse. I could have vegetable gardens and bill it as a farm-to-table kind of experience. Ecotourism is big right now, and it's only going to get bigger. People want to feel a connection to the land, and we could do that here. Hell, maybe we could get the orchard involved too. Apple-picking packages in the fall. And the barn—it's perfect for weddings. With the right decorator and caterers and the right marketing, it could be a huge hit."

He whirled around. "It would be crazy to buy this house, right? Tell me it would be crazy."

Mateus hated to agree, but it was. "It would be crazy," he said matter-of-factly.

Crawford's face fell.

Mateus hated that look. "But it couldn't hurt to call the Realtor and get a look inside. Maybe do a little research. You can't just open up a bed-and-breakfast on a whim."

Crawford grinned. "It isn't a whim. I mean, this location, yes. That's a whim. But I've always wanted my own place. I've been saving up to buy a place just like this for years. This is just a little sooner than I'd planned for it to happen. But I don't have a job, and if this place isn't too ridiculously priced, I have the money. I could give it a go. Do you mind if I call the Realtor now?" He waved his phone. "I have a signal up here at the house."

The thought of splitting up so soon after Crawford had arrived made Mateus's heart sink. Mateus didn't want to dampen Crawford's excitement, but he needed to get back to the orchard and had thought they could spend more time together there.

"I should go," Mateus said, holding back a sigh. "I need to make sure the hail hasn't damaged any of the trees. Do you think you can find your way back on your own?"

Crawford was already dialing. "Yeah. And if I can't, I'll call."

Mateus took a steadying breath and nodded. "Sure, okay. I'll take the basket back with me." And the blanket that was still covered in their come. Mateus was tempted to unroll it and check for proof that he hadn't imagined what had happened between them in the barn.

Wallowing wasn't going to get him anywhere, though, and he had work to do. Mateus didn't look back at Crawford as he set off through the trees. He'd thought having sex might make things clearer between them, but it had only muddied things further.

CRAWFORD had appeared just before dinner, flushed and ecstatic. While they ate, he'd talked a mile a minute about the details. He'd gone through the house with the Realtor, and he'd already talked to Adam about drawing up papers to buy it. He was certifiably insane, but Mateus seemed to be the only one who thought so.

Bree pulled up websites for four other ecotourism bed-and-breakfasts and had immediately started planning with Crawford. She'd been most excited about Crawford's idea to use the barn for weddings, though. Within an hour, she'd filled a Pinterest board with ideas for how they could decorate the space, and Crawford had hung on her every word.

Duarte had even offered to go over and take a look at the barn to see if it was usable or if it would need some work.

Mateus managed not to blush when Duarte had mentioned the barn, but it had been a near thing. He'd put the quilt in the washer the moment he'd walked in the door, and Bree had given him a sly, knowing look. Probably because he still had hay in his hair and his sweater had been on backward.

Mateus went upstairs early, unable to deal with the chatter about bamboo linens and whatever else Crawford and Bree were going on about. He'd spent a good three hours out in the orchard, picking up debris from the storm and restaking trees that had almost blown over, and all he wanted was a hot shower and bed.

Would it be awkward to share a bed with Crawford after what had happened between them? Mateus still had no idea where they stood, and it was eating at him. The mature thing to do would be to take Crawford aside and discuss it, but Mateus wasn't ready for that. It was possible—likely, even—that given his views on love and relationships, Crawford viewed Mateus as a hookup and nothing more. He'd been very clear that he needed Mateus's consent, but it hadn't been for anything more than sex.

It would be Mateus's own fault if he ended up heartbroken.

He took a too-hot shower, since he'd been unable to shake the chill of being caught out in the rain, and emerged tender and red but finally warm. One good thing about sleeping cuddled up with Crawford was their shared body heat, but Crawford was still downstairs. He could hear his voice drifting up the stairs, alternating with Bree's as they traded ideas back and forth.

Mateus put on a pair of boxers and slid between the cold sheets. They had a week until Officer Suarez came for their home visit, and after that, what? Would Crawford stay here if he bought that house? Or would it be an investment property that he had someone else run for him while he went back to LA?

As Mateus burrowed into his pillow, he wished he was still in the barn curled up on Crawford's chest, before things had gotten complicated and awkward.

He was still awake three hours later when Crawford tiptoed into the dark room, expertly avoiding the squeakiest floor planks and managing to get changed without turning on the light. Mateus wished they'd stayed in the guest room, because now he wouldn't be able to sleep in here without memories of what it was like to sleep in here with Crawford. Maybe he'd move into the guest room after they were done playing happy family for Officer Suarez.

Crawford climbed into bed behind him and curled his body around Mateus's, hooking his arm over Mateus's ribs. Mateus turned over so he could face him, hoping that maybe Crawford wanted to talk.

And he did, but not about them.

"I talked to Adam again, and he said all the paperwork looks good. The owners are desperate to sell. They moved to Florida last year, and the place has been empty ever since. The Realtor hired someone to take care of the grounds and keep up with the maintenance, so it's in really good shape. We scheduled a home inspector to come out in the morning, but if everything looks good, I'm going to sign the offer paperwork tomorrow afternoon."

"Isn't that fast?"

Crawford sighed dreamily, like a preteen with a heartthrob magazine. "It is. I know it is. But it just feels right. The right property, the right time. And since I don't need financing, I'll be able to close sooner. And they're letting me keep all the furniture, which is great because then I won't need to start from scratch."

"That's great. I'm really happy for you, if that's what you want."

Crawford shifted around so they were both lying on their backs, staring at the ceiling, shoulder to shoulder. "So Bree had an idea. And you can say no, but I think it's kind of perfect. Crazy, but perfect."

Mateus held his breath. After the day they'd had, he wasn't sure he wanted to know what Crawford would label as crazy.

"How about we have a vow renewal ceremony in the new barn during our home visit? It would show Officer Suarez that we're the real deal."

Would they be the real deal? Or were they still pretending? Before Mateus could ask, Crawford was talking again.

"And that way we'd be able to get started on promotional materials for the bed-and-breakfast too. Bree has a friend who's a commercial photographer, and she's free next Friday, so we could shoot the vow renewal and have some great shots to put out there. I won't be ready to open for guests for a few months, but most weddings are booked months if not a year or more in advance, so it's perfect timing."

And some weddings were planned an hour in advance, with rings purchased five minutes before the ceremony and witnesses pulled from the clerk's office.

Those didn't really count, though. At least, theirs didn't.

Mateus swallowed hard and tried to force himself to drift off to sleep with Crawford whispering in his ear about his plans. It was a far cry from the type of pillow talk he thought they'd be having, after their time together in the barn. The encounter obviously hadn't meant as much to Crawford as it had to him, and Mateus only had himself to blame for that. Crawford had made his views on marriage and love painfully clear over the last few weeks.

He curled in on himself tighter, willing his body to ignore the line of heat at his back where Crawford was touching him. Mateus had been naïve enough once to think that sex might change things between them, but he wasn't going to make that mistake a second time. He'd rushed things, and that was on him. He wouldn't do it again. Mateus was going to slow things down and do it right, but having Crawford so tantalizingly close was making that difficult.

Chapter Eighteen

Five days later

THEY'D run out of time to whitewash the inside of the barn, and Crawford was glad now they hadn't. The weathered wooden planks caught the shadows from the hanging lanterns beautifully, and paired with the way the spaces between the boards let in rays from the setting sun, the entire place had a soft, hazy glow. Someone had strung delicate white lights through the hayloft, crisscrossing them between the beams to illuminate the aisle down the middle of the barn, and it looked ethereal.

It was like nothing he'd seen before. All of the weddings he'd been to over the years had been beautiful in their own way, but they seemed sterile and cold compared to the breathtaking backdrop the barn provided. It felt homey and warm, and even though it was larger than some of the churches he'd been to ceremonies at, somehow the space was intimate and cozy. It was everything his first wedding hadn't been, and Crawford had to swallow past the growing lump in his throat and remind himself this was all just for show. They'd get some beautiful pictures out of the ceremony for the inn's brochure, and hopefully Officer Suarez would be satisfied enough by what she saw to leave them alone for a few months.

The catering crew they'd brought in was putting the finishing touches on the cake table, which was set up at the back of the barn. They weren't having a formal reception, just some dancing and drinks and a buffet of gorgeously rustic appetizers that Bree had delighted in helping them pick out. And the cake, of course. Crawford averted his eyes, not wanting to see them place the cake topper with its smiling grooms.

He nearly choked up when he saw the smile on Adam's face as he made his way down the aisle toward him. He was so lucky his brother had been able to join him, even though Brandon and Karen had already flown out to Japan.

Adam clapped him on the back. "Bro, I gotta say, you don't do things by half. Not only are you remarrying a total stranger, you're doing it in style—in the house you bought on a whim."

Crawford gave him a pained smile, and Adam's smirk slid off his face.

"What's up? Cold feet?" He looked around, his posture straightening when he saw the immigration officer declining a flute of champagne from a passing waiter. "It's a little late for a crisis of conscience, if that's what's happening."

Crawford huffed out a laugh. "No. But can I talk to you in the house for a minute?" The house was off-limits to wedding guests, since they'd focused all their efforts on getting the barn into shape for the wedding and the photo shoot. There were still holes in the floor upstairs, so they'd locked the doors to keep curious guests out. It was their only hope of finding any privacy amid the crowd milling around.

Adam shot a second glance over at the immigration officer, who had a small notebook out and was talking to Bree and another woman. "Are you asking to talk to your brother or your lawyer?"

"My brother."

"Then, yes, and it won't even cost you anything," Adam said, drawing a small smile out of Crawford.

Crawford jingled his keys. "Let's go into the house."

They'd been over at the house last night, but they'd been so busy setting up the postnup paperwork for Mateus to sign that they hadn't had time for much more than a cursory tour. Adam had to fly out in the morning, but Crawford was determined to find some time to give him a proper look around after the reception. They'd brought in a band, but that was mostly for the pictures. There would be a few cursory dances, and then they'd send everyone home.

Crawford and Adam ended up in the drawing room. The heavy brocade curtains were open, and Crawford could see the band setting up a dance floor in the yard. Beelzebub was on the windowsill, looking fat and happy in a slice of sunshine. He'd taken to the new house immediately, and there was already cat hair on most of the furniture.

"So what's up? Did Mateus change his mind about the postnup? I mean, you technically can sign and file that whenever, since the cat's already out of the bag marriagewise. But I'm strongly recommending you do it soon to shield your assets as best you can. It'll also shield him from the debt on this money pit, which I'm sure he'll appreciate."

Mateus was more in favor of the paperwork than Crawford was, which went a long way toward confirming Crawford's suspicion that they didn't actually need it. Though that was probably just his feelings for Mateus clouding the issue, and he was well acquainted with the fact that he couldn't trust his feelings.

"I'm not sure I can go through with any of this," Crawford blurted.

Adam gave him a puzzled look. "You already married him. This is just a show for the immigration officer and the cameras. And it looks great, man. You've got a gold mine with this idea. After these pictures are published, every hipster in a two-hundred-mile radius is going to be tripping over their hiking boots and skinny jeans to book this place."

"The vows, I mean."

Adam shot him a funny look. "You've already exchanged vows. You're literally promising the same things you've already promised."

"That's the problem," Crawford said, misery seeping through him.

Adam frowned. "You've lost me."

"My vows. I didn't mean them when we were married, so it wasn't a big deal. They were just words. But I'm falling in love with him. I do mean them now. And it's going to be so freaking obvious that I'm head over heels for him."

"Well, good. That's exactly what you want. You'll knock it out of the park for the immigration officer."

"No, I mean it. I'm fucked. He's gorgeous and modest and charming and perfect, and I'm absolutely and completely fucked."

"I thought the problem was you weren't," Adam joked. He sobered immediately when Crawford didn't laugh. "Ah, shit. You did. And then—what? Felt guilty about taking advantage and refused to talk about it? Bro. This was exactly what I was worried about when I asked you if you were sure about what you were getting yourself into."

Crawford rubbed a hand across his eyes. "It wasn't a problem when I married him. I didn't fall for him until later," he said wryly.

Adam made a sympathetic noise. "Don't shoot the messenger here, but are you sure you're not just confusing lust for feelings?"

"Lust is a feeling," Crawford said, his stomach turning sour. "And no. It's—I'm in way over my head. There's lust. But there's also a lot more."

"And you're sure you're alone in this? He seems to really like you."

A wave of guilt crashed through him, hot and sharp. Mateus had been distant since they'd had sex, and that was entirely his fault. He shouldn't have gotten carried away in the moment. They should have had a real talk before jumping in, and afterward Mateus had avoided him. It had made things pretty clear.

"That was for his brother's benefit," Crawford explained. "Duarte doesn't know this is all a sham. Mateus said his brother believes in true love, so our marriage of convenience would be deeply offensive."

Crawford was going to have to find another term for their relationship, because it certainly wasn't convenient. It didn't bother him that they'd married out of necessity, for practical reasons—he still didn't really care about the institution itself. He could take or leave being married to Mateus; it was Mateus himself that Crawford was having a hard time imagining living without.

"It's beyond ridiculous," he said. Maybe expressing it out loud would make it less true. Adam always accused him of being in his own head too much. Maybe getting it out there would help Crawford see reason. "We've only known each other a month. I can't possibly be in love with him."

"I don't think there's a rule book. Whether it's ridiculous or not, if it's what you're feeling, it's what you're feeling."

Crawford sneered. "When did you become Dr. Phil?"

"About the time you started channeling Nicholas Sparks."

Crawford gave Adam a sour look. "Ha, ha."

"Listen, it's your life. But Crawford? Maybe you don't recognize it because it's been so long since you've felt it, but you're happy. I haven't seen you like this in years. And maybe it's really selfish, but I'm glad. I hated the thought of leaving you alone."

Crawford snorted. "Japan isn't *that* far. I'll still see you. And I'm not alone. I have Beelzebub."

Adam didn't look convinced. "You like your stepdaddy, Bub?" he crooned, scratching behind Beelzebub's ears. Instead of snapping at him like he usually did, the cat started purring and rolled onto its back, exposing his belly. "Ah, you do, don't you? You have a big ol' crush on Mateus, just like your daddy does, don't you?"

Beelzebub let out a loud purr. Crawford had never seen him so relaxed and happy. Apparently he'd hated the sterile apartment as much as Crawford had. And he had really taken to Mateus. He'd even slept in Mateus's arms last night.

And Crawford had been jealous. Of his cat.

God, he was screwed.

Chapter Nineteen

IF Mateus could get through today, things would get better. Officer Suarez would be convinced he and Crawford were really together, and they could start actually moving on with their lives. Though that was going to be harder after Crawford opened his bed-and-breakfast….

Which was—something. A complication, to be sure. It would make their breakup harder on everyone. Everything would be so much easier if they could stage a fight and Crawford could disappear back to LA, but apparently nothing in Mateus's life was going to be easy.

Crawford had tried to talk to him a few times, but Mateus didn't need to hear the words come out of his mouth. He didn't want Crawford's pity or his lectures about love being a lie.

He wanted to wallow in his own hurt for a bit and then move on. Which was going to be a lot harder with his husband living next door. Granted, next door was actually five miles away. But Crawford and Bree got on like a house on fire, and half of Crawford's plans for his bed-and-breakfast involved the orchard. Mateus wasn't likely to get rid of him anytime soon.

Mateus didn't think he could bear it if Crawford gave him some condescending breakup speech. Especially since they'd never actually been together.

He sighed and examined himself in the mirror, then tugged on his bow tie. Luckily Bree had declared that tuxedos were too formal for a barn wedding, but that hadn't gotten him entirely out of dressing up. She'd forced him into a brown tweed suit that was too hot for the season and capped it off with the bright red bow tie he was struggling to straighten.

He had no idea what Crawford was wearing, but it was probably something devastatingly handsome.

Mateus sighed and gave up on his tie. Bree would fix it before the photographer got there.

Without even a cursory knock, Crawford opened the door and strode in, looking determined.

"I wanted to talk to you before—"

"I don't think you're supposed to see the groom before the wedding. It's bad luck."

Crawford quirked an eyebrow at him. "Since we're already married, I don't think that holds any water."

Mateus shrugged. "I need to go down and make sure the chairs are right. And that the band is setting up in the right place."

"Duarte and Adam are taking care of that. I—"

Mateus held up a hand, cutting him off. "I know, all right? You made it clear. I don't need you to spell it out for me. I'd rather we not do this today, okay? You can tell me all about how it was a mistake and you regret it later, but let's just get through the wedding first. I won't—I'm not expecting anything of you. I get it."

While Crawford stood there in stunned silence, Mateus stalked to the door and left. He'd go hide in the back of the barn until they were ready for him.

EVERYTHING about the ceremony had been choreographed, including who Officer Suarez was going to sit with.

Mateus and Crawford would walk down the aisle together, and there would be a short ceremony and then the reception. Crawford looked pale and shaky when Mateus met him outside the barn, but he offered Mateus a small smile, so it must not be regrets. Probably nerves, thanks to Officer Suarez.

They made it down the aisle without a problem, but Crawford surprised everyone when he went off script and took Mateus's hands in his before he dropped down to one knee when they got to the front. The justice of the peace shifted. "Usually we do this part standing up, gentlemen," he said with an uncomfortable chuckle.

Mateus couldn't take his eyes off Crawford, who was staring up at him with a small, expectant grin on his face. He glanced over at the justice of the peace and winked. "I'll just be a moment," he said before turning his full attention back to Mateus.

"Will you marry me?" he asked, his gaze intent. His voice was clear and strong, but Mateus could feel tiny tremors going through Crawford's hands. Crawford was nervous, yes. But maybe not about Officer Suarez. About… him?

A thrill shot up his spine, and Mateus was sure his own hands were shaking too. The barn was dead silent, and he kept his eyes locked on Crawford, not wanting to look around and see everyone watching them. "I believe I already have."

Their guests laughed, and Crawford cracked a smile and squeezed Mateus's hands.

"True. But we missed out on this part, and I didn't want you to regret not having a real proposal in twenty years when we're telling our niece about our wedding." The tone was jovial, like he was joking, but he wasn't. Crawford was actually asking Mateus to marry him. To spend their lives together.

Mateus's heart was in his throat, and he wasn't sure he'd be able to speak without letting a sob escape. He nodded instead.

Crawford clucked his tongue softly. "I need words, Mateus. You haven't given me any, and this is your choice. I didn't do a good job of this here in this barn before, and I want to fix that. I didn't mean for that to be a onetime thing. I meant it when I said I wanted you. You. All of you, for all of time," he said, his tone hushed. No one beyond the front row would know what he'd said, and the significance wasn't lost on Mateus. The immigration officer was in the back. If Mateus didn't want this—for real, not just on paper—then all he had to do was say no. Crawford wouldn't call a halt to the ceremony or divorce him. He wasn't the kind of man who'd go back on his word. Even if Mateus refused his offer to make their fake marriage a real one, Crawford would do the honorable thing and fulfil his commitment to save Mateus from deportation.

Instead, he was the type who proposed a genuine marriage to his own husband on bended knee during their very public vow renewal.

"Yes," Mateus managed to rasp out. "Yes, I'll marry you. Of course I will. I love you."

Crawford's entire body stiffened at Mateus's admission, and a look of pure joy lit his face. "I love you too."

Mateus was definitely shaking now. Crawford stood, still holding Mateus's hands, their arms at awkward angles as he pulled him closer and kissed him sweetly on the mouth.

The justice of the peace coughed. "Again, doing things a little out of order, gentlemen," he said, laughter in his voice this time.

Crawford stepped back but didn't let go of Mateus's hands. "Sorry. We're ready now," he said, his eyes never leaving Mateus's. Mateus let out a watery laugh, and he heard Bree start to sob in the front row.

"All right, then," the justice of the peace said. "Ladies and gentlemen, we are gathered here today to witness the renewal of vows between Crawford Hargrave and Mateus Fontes. I have to say, I've presided over dozens of weddings, but none that are quite this unique. These gentlemen were married in Vancouver almost a month ago, and they've chosen to renew their vows here in front of their friends and family. I'm honored to be a part of it, since it's obvious how much love there is between them."

Bree sighed dreamily from her spot next to Duarte, and Mateus had to bite back a hysterical laugh. This was all surreal. From the twinkling fairy lights that crisscrossed the barn to the sweet-musty scent of the hay that lingered in the air, it was all perfect. Battery-operated candles flickered in the Mason jars he and Duarte had painstakingly hung from the rafters an hour earlier, though that felt like a lifetime ago. He'd been worried about getting through his vows without all of his emotions written across his face, and now he was beaming so hard it hurt, his happiness radiating out of him and reflecting right back at him from Crawford. Mateus hadn't realized it was even possible to feel this happy.

"Crawford and Mateus, marriage is a sacred rite. It joins two people together to walk the same road. It's a very special thing to find two people who will vow to see each other through life's challenges and joys. We celebrate that love and commitment with you here today."

The words weren't that different from the ones they'd heard in the clerk's office in Vancouver, but this time Mateus felt them resonate in his bones. He and Crawford might've already been married on paper, but this, *this* was their wedding day.

The justice of the peace held his hands out. "Bree, Duarte, and Adam, would you please step forward?"

Both Mateus and Crawford had been hesitant when they'd talked about including this family blessing in the ceremony. Mateus hadn't wanted to drag their families deeper into the lie, but both Bree and Duarte had been so excited at the prospect of being included that he hadn't been able to say no. Now he was glad they'd allowed themselves to be railroaded into it.

Duarte reached out and clasped his hand around Mateus's elbow, and Adam did the same with Crawford's. Bree's belly bumped against Mateus's hip as she placed her hand over top of Mateus's and Crawford's joined hands. It felt right, like his niece was part of things.

"A marriage joins not only two people but two families," the justice of the peace said. "Bree, Duarte, and Adam, do you promise to support these men and their marriage, providing comfort and support when they need it, and welcoming Crawford and Mateus into your families?"

"We do," they said in unison. Duarte squeezed Mateus's elbow before stepping back into line behind him with Bree and Adam.

Mateus swallowed hard, tears pricking at the corners of his eyes. He'd never thought of himself as particularly sappy, but apparently he'd been wrong.

"Crawford, a month ago you vowed to take Mateus as your husband. Will you continue to have him as your lawfully wedded husband?"

Crawford's voice was hoarse as he answered. "I will."

Mateus's knees wobbled as the justice of the peace turned his gaze on him. "Mateus, a month ago you vowed to take Crawford as your husband. Will you continue to have him as your lawfully wedded husband?"

Mateus's throat was as dry as the Sahara, but he managed to croak out his affirmation. "I will."

"Crawford, do you reaffirm your love for Mateus? Will you continue to honor, love, and cherish him as your partner and your equal, forsaking all others and promising your faithfulness as long as you both shall live?"

Crawford pinned Mateus with a heated gaze that had Mateus trembling with more than just nerves. "I will."

"Mateus, do you reaffirm your love for Crawford? Will you continue to honor, love, and cherish him as your partner and your equal, forsaking all others and promising your faithfulness as long as you both shall live?"

This had been the part of their original vows that Mateus had felt the guiltiest about in Vancouver, but he wholeheartedly pledged himself to it now.

"I will," he said, his lips quirking up into a smile when Crawford's fingers tightened on his where they were still joined.

"You exchanged rings as an outward symbol of your love and as a reminder of the promises you made on your wedding day. Please join your left hands together now."

It was an awkward shuffle, and they ended up with Crawford's hand on top.

"Crawford, please repeat after me: Mateus, I wear this ring as a symbol of my love and commitment to you."

Crawford's fingers twitched, and Mateus flicked his gaze between the ring Crawford had bought for himself and his face. "Mateus, I wear this ring as a symbol of my love and commitment to you."

"Now, please switch your hands, with Mateus's on top. Mateus, please repeat after me: Crawford, I wear this ring as a symbol of my love and commitment to you."

Mateus cleared his throat. His voice was stronger than it had been a moment ago. "Crawford, I wear this ring as a symbol of my love and commitment to you."

"Marriage is a conscious choice, one you must reaffirm every day of your lives. May these rings serve as a reminder of your love for each other and the love that joins you together," the justice of the peace said. "Crawford and Mateus, today you have reaffirmed your vows to each other. You have joined yourselves and your families together, and you leave here today greater for it. May you have a happy, love-filled marriage."

He put a hand on both of their shoulders, and Mateus shifted a step closer to Crawford. Crawford's eyes followed him hungrily, his attention centered on Mateus's mouth. Mateus had to fight the urge to lick his lips, knowing what was coming next.

The justice of the peace patted them both on the back and flashed them a huge smile. "Thank you for allowing us to bear witness and celebrate the occasion of your vow renewal. The ties that bind you are stronger than ever. If you so choose, you may mark this milestone with a kiss."

Mateus didn't think there was any power on earth that could have stopped them from doing just that. He leaned in, and a shiver ran down his spine when Crawford's warm lips touched his. They were chapped because Crawford bit his bottom lip when he was nervous. He'd probably chewed it nearly raw working himself up to the proposal. It was endearing.

Their left hands were still joined, which made Mateus's shoulder twinge when he pushed even closer to deepen the kiss. He kept it chaste, mindful of the audience, but he couldn't resist running his tongue along the seam of Crawford's lips, soothing over the rough skin.

Everyone broke into raucous applause when they pulled apart. Crawford let go of his hand, but Mateus didn't have much time to worry over the loss before Crawford was pulling him into a tight embrace and pressing another soft kiss against his neck. "I love you," he murmured, just loud enough for Mateus to hear him. "I do. It's the craziest thing I've ever done, but it's true."

"Crazier than marrying me a few hours after you met me?" Mateus whispered as Crawford pulled back and grinned at him, his entire face shining. "Well, I love you too, so I guess we're both crazy."

Crawford twined their hands together, and they made their way down the aisle and out the open barn doors.

They'd need to go back for pictures soon, but Mateus wanted a little time with Crawford before they had to talk to other people. He led him down the gravel drive, away from the crowd.

"I'm sorry I didn't listen earlier," Mateus said when they'd gotten far enough away. They were still holding hands, and as far as Mateus was concerned he might never let go.

"I'm sorry I didn't notice you were upset until it was too late. I'm not always good with words and emotions."

Crawford pulled him to a stop, and Mateus looked up and laughed when he realized they were under the trees they'd hidden from the rain under. It felt like ages ago, but it had only been a little less than a week. Things had been surreal lately.

"So, just to be clear, we're married now," Crawford said, his eyes sparkling.

Mateus couldn't help but laugh. "We were married before too."

"Ah, but now we're going to consummate it. So we'll be *married*."

"Are we?"

Crawford's smile deepened. "We are. And we're going to do it again and again, just to make sure it took."

"I'm not sure it works like that, but I'm willing to go along with it."

Crawford nuzzled against Mateus's neck.

"That was a hell of a first kiss up there," he murmured.

"We've kissed before."

Crawford pulled back, and the intense look on his face made Mateus's chest flare with heat. "It's not—yes. We've kissed before," he said, knocking his forehead against Mateus's as they both laughed. "But it wasn't real. I mean, not like this. Not for keeps. So I want that to be our first kiss. The first one where it really meant something."

Mateus swallowed hard and brought a hand up to stroke Crawford's cheek. It was the cleanest shaven Mateus had ever seen him. He was touched how much trouble Crawford had gone to in order to look nice for their wedding, but the truth was Mateus kind of missed the stubble. A smile ghosted across Crawford's lips at the light touch.

"They all meant something," Mateus said. "I never once touched you without it meaning something to me. I wouldn't."

Crawford blinked hard and looked away for a minute. "I didn't always give you a choice. That first time, at the border—"

"It was a comfort."

Mateus had never tried so hard to look earnest in his entire life. He needed Crawford to know he was all in, and that he'd never felt forced. "You've been what I needed from the second I saw you at the airport, arguing with the clerk."

Crawford managed a wet-sounding laugh. "I wasn't arguing with anyone. I was very polite."

"So polite that you couldn't let a stranger be arrested at the border for an expired visa."

"Well," Crawford said, leaning in to press a kiss to Mateus's throat. "The stranger in question was tall, dark, and handsome. He made a good impression."

"And without you I'd have been tall, dark, and deported."

Crawford made a hurt noise in his throat. "Don't even joke about that. You're mine, and I'm never letting you go."

Mateus felt like his heart was about to beat out of his chest. "I love you."

"It doesn't matter how we met, or why we got married. All that matters is that I'm in love with you, and I want you by my side no matter where I go."

This time when Crawford kissed him, there was no hesitation, no doubt. It felt like coming home.

Coming in May 2017

#33

Stage Two by Ariel Tachna

Love has a steep learning curve.

Assistant high-school principal Blake Barnes has everything he wants: a chance to help troubled students and an outlet for his passion for theater. Well, almost everything—he still goes home to an empty apartment. Then his high-school crush explodes back into his life, the unexpected guardian of two boys in Blake's care.

Thane Dalton has always been a bad boy through and through. Not much has changed, including his mistrust of authority figures, and no amount of institutional bureaucracy will keep him from protecting his nephews from the bullies terrorizing them. If that means butting heads with Blake, so be it.

Blake and Thane have lessons to learn: that they both have the boys' best interests at heart, that the tension between them isn't just confrontational, and that sparks can fly when opposites come together.

#34

Two for Trust by Elle Brownlee

American nurse Finch Mason steps beyond the comfort of his orderly life and takes a dream trip to England, complete with a National Trust Pass so he can visit numerous historical sites. At the first one his list, he's warmly welcomed—and told he bought a pass good for two.

Finch doesn't hesitate to offer the pass to Benedict, a handsome Brit also there on an outing. They spend a magical week touring the countryside, and while it's too soon to get attached, Finch wishes their time together would never end.

Then Finch finds himself stuck abroad with no money, and he has no one to turn to but Benedict. Benedict is happy to help, but he also owes Finch some answers—such as who he really is and why he was at the estate where they first met.

Now Available

#29

Snowblind by Eli Easton

Snow, steam, and secrets.

The latest snowstorm carries something unexpected to the doorstep of Hutch's secluded Alaskan cabin: a stranger named Jude, the most beautiful man Hutch has ever seen. Jude says he's in the area for a ski trip, and that he fled a domineering lover, thinking he could make it into town. But Hutch is a suspicious SOB and treats his unwanted guest warily. The problem is Jude isn't just gorgeous, he's funny and smart and flirtatious.

Two gay men snowed in for three days—things happen. Really good things. By the time the storm clears, Hutch finds himself a little too attached to Jude Devereaux, San Francisco-based male model. But is Jude what he claims to be? Or is he entangled in the secrets Hutch moved to Alaska to escape?

#30

Two Cowboys and a Baby by BA Tortuga

A little bundle of joy means big changes.

Hoss McMasters has a working ranch, a bull riding career, a nosy momma, and a best friend who he's been in love with since he can remember. He's a busy, happy cowboy living the good life.

Then one morning he discovers a baby on his doorstep.

Well, Hoss does what any reasonable man would do—he calls his momma and his buddy, Sheriff Pooter, and they head to the clinic to see if Doc knows of any suddenly not-so-pregnant girls.

In the meantime, he and his best friend, Bradley, have their hands full trying to care for an infant, run a ranch, and deal with the sudden confession that Bradley doesn't hate Hoss for coming out to him in high school. In fact, Bradley's been trying to catch Hoss's attention for damn near a decade.

www.dreamspinnerpress.com